SEND HIM VICTORIOUS

BOOK 2

by Bart Cline

UNDERSTATED PRODUCTIONS

Published by Understated Productions 2016
Copyright © 2016 by Bart Cline
www.bartcline.me

Published in Great Britain
ISBN 978-1545311677

Typeset in Minion Pro by Understated Productions
Printed by CreateSpace

Contents

BOOK TWO

1

Rehabilitation

"The Security Council will now begin its consideration of item two of the agenda," the representative from Uruguay, who for this month was also the President of the United Nations Security Council, said. "Mr Achille, you have the floor."

Philippe Achille, a swarthy Mediterranean-looking man of about retirement age, held a sheet of paper and wore gold reading glasses. The desk-plaque identifying him to the other representatives and the television cameras marked him as the Under-Secretary-General. "Mr President," he said in French, "in the ongoing discussion concerning the so-called New Order of Great Britain and Northern Ireland, the Security Council must consider its actions carefully. As a founding member of the United Nations, the United Kingdom has long been a valued voice in these chambers. Her advice and actions have generally been balanced, sensible, tending toward human rights, and carefully considered, rarely acting rashly or with undue fervour."

The blue chairs surrounding the Council Chamber's horseshoe-shaped conference table were occupied by representatives of all but one of the member states: the United Kingdom's seat was empty. The representative for Turkmenistan, occupying the seat to the left, had draped his coat over the UK chair, and the Representative for Cameroon, at the right, had allowed his notes, pens, and laptop accessories to spread onto the UK desk space.

The monumental cubist painting by a now-largely-forgotten Norwegian artist loomed over the chamber, dominating the attention of any who sat in the rows of spectator seating directly opposite, even though the council's deliberations took place between the two. At either side of the painting were curtains hanging the entire height of the chamber, some ten metres, covering windows through which none of the delegates had ever seen the East River or even the sun.

"But her actions at the present time, and her present government, must be carefully considered before the Security Council can decide whether to re-admit the United Kingdom to her place in this august body."

King Alfred stood behind his desk. General Montgomery, wearing a civilian suit instead of his usual uniform, occupied a chair on the opposite side of the desk, listening to and watching the King. A tablet computer was propped up on the desk, displaying a live BBC news report.

A voice came from a speakerphone. "And they just turfed me out!"

"I know they did," Alfred said. "I've just seen it on the BBC! Why have you waited so long to report it?"

"It only just happened, Your Majesty! The journalists and camera-people were already there. They still are! The reporters can get in, but I can't."

"You have a Royal warrant. Assert yourself, man!"

"I'm sorry Your Majesty, but you're going to have to behead me or something, because I can't get back in there. Security escorted me out, and two of New York City's finest are right here, making sure I don't try anything."

"Very well Mr Snelling. I need to think about this. We'll talk again very soon." The King touched the hang-up button. "Well Stewart, this is an unprecedented position, is it not?"

"What, being thrown out of the Security Council? Britain is a 'permanent member'. Rather makes a mockery of the language, doesn't it? Well, so much for our power of veto. Definitely unexpected."

"Unprecedented, Stewart, but not unexpected. It was always a possibility. Ours is the first of the Security Council's permanent members to have undergone a complete change of government."

"Really, Your Majesty? What about Russia?"

"No. Russia may have moved away from communism, but it's still ruled from the same place by more or less the same people. Despite massive changes, it still has a continuity of government. No, we're the first. Rule has been taken away from Westminster and transferred to the Palace."

"Yes. The New Order."

"Exactly."

"If you're not surprised by this," Montgomery said, "then you must have a plan. A way to make them pay. This insult to Britain – and to you! – can't be let pass."

"I do have a plan old friend. But not to get even. That is not the proper way to do international relations."

"'Proper ways' be hanged! This amounts to a declaration of war! So get off your arse, and–" The General looked at his chair, and stood up. "–and… and… There are ways. Our SAS boys will have some grisly ideas what to do with these UN vermin."

Montgomery swayed, his eyes glazing over while sweat ran down his face.

Lindsey appeared next to the General, putting a hand on the officer's shoulder, which the older man slapped away.

"And I suppose, Your Majesty, that you also foresaw the civil war?"

Lindsey was on the phone, speaking quietly. "Doctor, would you come to the King's office right away? Thank you." He hung up.

"Indeed I did," the King continued. "But sometimes one thinks one is ready for something – only to find that, when it actually comes to pass, one is not as ready as one thought after all."

"Well, I'd have been ready." The General was almost shouting. "You should have warned me. I would have crushed the… the… swine by now!"

A knock came at the door, which Lindsey answered immediately. "Doctor Jimpson, thank you for coming so quickly. The General isn't well."

"Ah," Jimpson said as he set down his medical bag, "what's ailing you General?"

"Nothing is ailing me, you pathetic nose-hair. Fit as a fiddle! Now get out. I'm trying to advise the King, and you're on the verge of being arrested for interfering with foreign policy!"

"Doctor," Alfred said, "sedate him."

"Ah. I'm sorry General, but His Majesty's just pulled rank on you." Jimpson opened his bag and prepared a syringe.

"Now, sit down Stewart." The King made sure to stand his full height, imposing himself over Montgomery.

Montgomery began to comply, until he saw Jimpson's syringe. Lashing out like the trained fighter he was, the General knocked over the King and Dr Jimpson before looking at Lindsey.

Lindsey dropped his pens and notebook and dashed out the door.

Remaining on the floor for the moment, the King and Jimpson looked up at Montgomery, whose face was red and eyes wild, swaying with confusion, teeth bared, fists clenched.

Lindsey returned with three soldiers. They looked at the King on the floor, and at the angry Montgomery.

The soldiers grappled with the General, succeeding in restraining him.

"Now, Doctor," the King said, getting up off the floor.

Jimpson wasted no time complying, regaining his feet as he recovered the dropped syringe.

Again, on seeing it, the General struggled against the soldiers' grip, but they held him fast.

"I'm only giving you a sedative, General. It won't do you any harm." The Doctor injected the General. "Your Majesty, he's suffering from severe post-traumatic stress. As you can see from his face, he hasn't had an easy time in captivity. When I examined him yesterday I found numerous other superficial injuries, consistent with… well, torture. His captors certainly had a go at him."

"I want you to do whatever you can for him. If his psyche is outside your area of expertise, let's bring in a specialist."

"He's probably not going to want to talk about it, and it probably wouldn't do any good to try to force him. I've seen enough of these old soldiers. I know how they tick. I feel certain he'll get better, though how soon depends entirely on him. You were probably right to ease him back into work, Your Majesty, but… well… I don't know. His sort hates to recuperate. Come on, General, you'd better get some rest."

Dr Jimpson led the now-compliant Montgomery out of the King's office.

"Get him back on his feet, Doctor. He has important work to do."

"Surely, Your Majesty, his health comes first."

"Doctor, have you not seen the news recently? The nation's health comes first."

Jimpson deflated with a sigh. "As you wish, Your Majesty." He left, helping the disoriented General along.

The Doctor exited the room.

Alfred let his breath out in a deep sigh, emptying his lungs, as he rubbed his eyes vigorously with his palms.

"Are you all right Your Majesty?"

"Yes Sergeant," the King said, brushing dust off of his sleeves. "You may return to your duties."

"Very good sir." The soldier saluted Alfred, and departed.

"Well Blair, it's just you and me now."

"Yes, Your Majesty," Lindsey said. "And that lot out there – and the rest of the armed services, and a lot of the general public – are with you."

"Mmm. Nevertheless, I do rather depend on Stewart. I need him back to full capacity as soon as possible, and Jimpson – as good a medic as he is – is not the man to do it. Stewart isn't injured; he's traumatised, and that needs a different sort of doctor."

"Do you want me to find a good psychologist? If such a creature exists?"

"I already have such a person in mind. Dr Sperry. Do you know him?"

"Of him, yes." Lindsey crinkled his brow. "A lot of people do, since his picture was on the front of the Daily Mail. Disbarred, as I recall. Malpractice."

"Disbarrment is for lawyers. But essentially correct." Alfred puffed his cheeks out, exhaling. "And his is exactly the sort of malpractice we require just now."

"The patient is highly resistant," Dr Sperry said, his face bruised and bloodied. When he took a drink from his small glass medicine bottle a swirl of blood mingled with the clear liquid. He put the lid on and twisted it shut.

Sperry was tall and lean, and could easily be mistaken for a thug if met on the street. Middle-aged and fearsome-looking, he wore a white lab coat, now flecked with red. His short grey hair was a mess, along with his clothes.

Standing behind the King, Lindsey's jaw hung open as he observed Sperry's brutalised features. The disbarred doctor appeared not to notice the strange contrast between his battered appearance and the tasteful decor of the Garden Room, despite it still bearing marks of the firefight which had recently taken place there. The place remained elegant, even bearing the scar where a hole had been torn through the wall when the General was extracted by the insurgents.

"Did General Montgomery do that to you?" Lindsey asked.

"Of course, son," Sperry replied. "There's no one else in the treatment room."

"But why?"

"My method is to push the patient to violence, by verbal abuse, frustration, circular reasoning, and so on. It's much faster than encouraging him to talk out his problems and, I believe, more permanent."

"But surely it'll traumatise him even more. Since when is violence to be encouraged as a way of solving your personal problems?"

"My record speaks for itself. I don't have time right now to explain the theories behind my therapeutic method. Get my book if you want to know more. Of course, it's on the banned list, but…"

"That is absolutely appalling," Lindsey said, aghast. "Where's the room for kindness in your method?"

"How dare you impugn my capacity for kindness, boy. Am I not being kind by allowing someone in need to vent his considerable pent-up rage on my own body? He'll be the better for it. Cured even."

"Allowing him to brutalise you is no kindness."

"Blair," the King said, "this is not the time for moralising. These are not methods I would condone if the need were not great."

"Let me just say this," Sperry said. "I always get an apology after they see how I've helped them. Even a hug and some tears. When I see them resuming normal life and fully cured, it is worth every moment. I'll get back to my patient now."

Sperry exited.

"I fail to see what you're so upset about, Blair. His method is remarkably similar to your Christian Atonement, surely."

"Clearly, you do not understand that doctrine, Your Majesty. The Atonement is the pure for the impure, the sinless for the sinner, the love of the Creator for the creature. Sperry's so-called 'method' is more like a sick parody. It's disgusting."

Alfred's features sagged. "I do, in fact, agree with you. But I find my options are limited by circumstances."

Lindsey shook his head. "It's disgusting."

"I hope this incident doesn't shake your service to me, old friend. Or your faith."

"No, Your Majesty. In the words of the Apostle, 'troubled on every side, yet not distressed; perplexed, but not in despair; cast down, but not destroyed'. I serve Christ because he has the words of eternal life. I serve you because you're my King. And you pay my salary."

"Very well."

"But," Lindsey said, rubbing the stubble on his chin, "please consider this my formal protest."

"So noted," the King said, pointing at Lindsey's notebook. "And so note it."

2

Negotiation

"**Y**ou cannot possibly be serious, Father." Adrian, the Prince of Wales, spoke with a defiant tone, though he palpitated, brow crinkled, eyes glazed. "After what happened in Scotland? I thought your notion of sending me to Brussels was mad – thank goodness that never went forward – but this… You want me to turn the United Nations against us now! No! I won't even think about it."

"I understand, son," the King said, putting his hand on Adrian's shoulder, feeling his son's tense and quivering muscles. "You've been disheartened. I know that. You see Scotland as your failure. But your shipmates have informed me of the dignity you possessed as you entered Edinburgh, the speech you prepared and the conviction with which you delivered it. And Captain Roberts has told me how you've become much better company of late."

"Yes, I've begun to recover and rebuild." The Prince shuddered. "Now you want to ruin all that! Repeat the whole fiasco."

"The United Nations is not Scotland. It's an entirely different animal. The Scottish Parliament has three parties, and therefore three purposes. The UN has a hundred and eighty nine parties, and therefore a hundred and eighty nine purposes. 'Commonality' is a word they have yet to translate into the official language of the UN. Therefore, you have only to persuade a few."

"Well, that's as may be. But in your heart didn't you think the same thing about Scotland? And look what happened."

"I can't predict everything. It may come as something of a shock to you that I'm only human." The King smiled, baring his perfectly-aligned teeth as he gripped his son's shoulder.

Adrian let out a deep breath he had been holding, also smiled, and relaxed his posture. "Perhaps you're right."

Alfred offered his right hand to his son.

Adrian made a tentative move, slowly extending his hand toward his father's.

With only a millimetre between their hands, the Prince withdrew his and turned away.

"Why not send Frances? She's more erudite, more educated, more dedicated than I am. She'd be a fine ambassador."

The King sighed. "I don't need an ambassador. I need the heir to the throne."

"But the UN are out for blood. I don't want to be the sacrificial lamb."

"If anyone else is allowed to galvanise their political will," Alfred said, turning to allow Adrian to look at him again, "it will go badly for us. I have to send them my son. Only that will persuade them." The King took his son by the shoulders, looking him directly in the eyes. "Only you can persuade them."

Adrian tensed, breath shallow, pupils dilated. He examined his father's eyes, staring into them as if peering into the older man's mind.

Exhaling deeply, the Prince's muscles slackened, the furrows in his forehead vanished.

A sympathetic expression, indistinguishable from hope, played over the King's face.

"Very well. I'll go to New York for you."

The King, only for a moment, extended his hands toward the Prince, as if to offer a hug, but let his left hand drop to his side, leaving his right extended. The Prince shook it.

"Thank you," the King said, "Your Highness."

"You're welcome, Your Majesty." The Prince allowed his lips to relax into a shadow of a smile. "After all, what have I really got to lose?"

***

As the HMS Dominance lay in Plymouth harbour, it had received as much fresh paint as there had been time for. The crew had been expending every effort to ensure that the Prince's return to his ship would be pleasant and encouraging.

The King had impressed upon Captain Dickie Roberts the importance of making the Prince feel as at-home and comfortable as was humanly possible. Roberts had insisted that they were already doing a great deal toward that end, and that they would continue to do so.

The Prince's limousine, having passed a large number of well-wishers along the streets of the city, as well as a smaller number of ill wishers, stopped near the ship's gangway.

David, the Prince's bodyguard, exited the limousine first, holding the door open for his boss.

Stepping out of his vehicle, the Prince saluted the several officers and crew who had stood waiting for him for at least as long as it took him to drive between the harbour's security gates and the ship.

Crossing the gangway to the door he came to a stop opposite the Captain, who stood waiting for him. The two men saluted one another.

"Permission to come aboard, Dickie?"

"Granted, Your Highness." Roberts completed his salute as the Prince boarded the ship.

Together they made their way to the bridge, pausing frequently to salute officers and ratings who were passing in the performance of their duties.

"Captains on the bridge!" Commander Indrani led the bridge crew in standing to attention.

"At ease, men," the Prince said as he looked at Commander Indrani, "and ladies."

Naval pleasantries were exchanged.

"So," Indrani said, looking at the Prince, "what are our new orders, Captain?"

"We sail to New York…"

Looks of confusion were exchanged between the sailors.

"Isn't that rather far from the action, sir?" Indrani said.

"... to the United Nations," the Prince continued.

Murmurs and looks of understanding dawned on the crew members.

"In that case Sir, we'll be honoured to represent the King in New York."

"Excellent, Jasmina. Dickie, how soon can you have us in New York?"

"I think we should be able to do it in seven days, Your Highness."

"Can you make it six?"

The Captain half-smiled. "That shouldn't be a problem sir. Of course, we might need to throw all your luggage overboard…"

The Prince returned the half-smile. "In that case, we set off as soon as we receive clearance from the port authorities. Now, if you'll excuse me, I'll see you all at dinner tonight. I've got to go unpack my things." He turned to the door.

"Actually, Your Highness," Indrani said, "your… er… cabin boy is taking care of that for you even as we speak."

"Well, that is a pleasant surprise." The Prince held his hands together in front of his abdomen, and twiddled his thumbs. "That's a couple of hours freed up. I don't know what I'm going to do with myself."

"You could join me in my quarters for a cognac," Roberts said.

"Very well Dickie. Though I don't think this is really the time for me to be drinking you under the table. Don't you need to be on the bridge to steer?"

"The Commander's perfectly capable of taking us out of port."

Captain Roberts issued his orders, and he and the Prince left the bridge.

The journey took six days, as planned.

During the course of which, the ship encountered a heavy but short storm, through which the Captain merely applied full power.

The Prince had, on at least three occasions, attempted to seduce Commander Indrani, but she was adept at rebuffing his advances in a kindly but firm manner which only made him desire her more.

The Prince had also made advances to a number of the other female crew members, but met with limited success. Because he was old enough to be a father to even the most mature sea-women on board, they appeared not to take his romantic efforts seriously.

He also spent a lot of time talking and drinking with Captain Roberts, with whom he had many things in common. Not the least of these was his philandering tendencies. The Captain's one saving grace in this area was that he had no designs on the female members of his crew, but rather kept a girl – or girls – in every port, which he said forced him to ration himself and gave him something to look forward to. And, like the Prince, the Captain enjoyed a frequent tipple, having a drink as often as he could without it affecting his judgement – and his tolerance for alcohol was considerable. On one occasion the Prince commented, "It seems to me there's more virtue in the ranks than there is at the top." To which the Captain smiled and agreed.

On occasion however, Commander Indrani sat with the Prince at meals, of her own volition and to his mild surprise.

Having very little actual work to do, Adrian also spent much time with the ratings, usually taking his lunch with them. He found he enjoyed their generally coarse language and unrefined behaviour. He even found himself sympathising with their hardships, whether maintaining a wife and children while living the life of a sailor, making ends meet on a navy salary, or keeping their multiple girlfriends from learning about one another. In his capacity as a sailor was the only time he ever spent with the common man, and this was his first tour of duty in a long time.

***

Slightly ahead of schedule, the Dominance arrived in New York harbour. The crew enjoyed seeing the Statue of Liberty and parking the ship under the shadow of the city's forest of skyscrapers, whetting their appetite for shore leave – which was restricted to only a couple of hours per sailor on account of the fact that they would not know how long they were staying in port until the Prince concluded his business at the UN.

The Prince, dressed in a smart navy-blue suit with a burgundy tie, entered the limousine the United Nations had sent for him.

The New York Police Department provided an escort of motorcycles, keeping the street clear for some distance ahead and behind.

Having none of his own bodyguard available to him here, the Prince reassured himself that he would be safe in the care of New York's finest.

That the United Nations had sent a car for him led him to believe he would be well received, but upon arrival in the gated United Nations compound a welcoming committee was conspicuous by its absence. The limousine parked outside the conference building, inside which the Security Council met, and only the driver escorted him in.

Once inside the building, the Prince was subjected to a standard security screening by apologetic but unimpressed guards, which led him to wonder if the United Nations now saw the Prince of Wales as a potential terrorist.

Accompanied into the Security Council chamber by two uniformed security guards, Adrian was directed to sit down in the United Kingdom's seat, the very seat which had only a week before been vacated by Britain's designated representative.

The adjacent representatives removed their coats from the empty chair and their accessories from the unoccupied desk space as Adrian approached.

Not allowed to interrupt the proceedings, the Prince sat as patiently as he could while the current business was wound up. After perhaps an hour it was his turn. The president of the Security Council conducted the formalities, introduced the Prince, and gave him the floor.

Behind each seat surrounding the horseshoe-shaped conference table were four similar chairs, each fixed to the floor. Many of the delegates sitting behind the representatives balanced notebooks or tablet computers on their laps. Behind the Prince sat four local consular functionaries whose names he did not know.

Standing – having perhaps failed to notice that no other delegates stood to speak, nor the fixed microphone on the table – the Prince spoke, projecting his confident voice across the large room so that even without amplification everyone in the chamber could hear him.

"Mr President, Mr Under-Secretary, I am here to seek redress for an injustice against the United Kingdom, perpetrated here, in this very chamber."

Overlooking the chamber on either side were windows behind which were the technicians' booths, where the public address system was managed and translation streams fed to the appropriate delegates' earpieces. Frantic with activity, the group of technicians moved their hands over controls on mixing desks with practiced fervour as they argued.

"Boost his mike to max!"

"I can't. Feedback."

"Why won't he sit down?"

"Can we get a parabolic on him?"

"Through this glass?"

"Do we even have a parabolic?"

Prince Adrian, still beginning his speech, cut himself off in mid-sentence. He tapped the microphone which at the moment reached only as high as his waist. The loudspeakers boomed.

The technicians breathed a sigh of relief as the Prince of Wales sat down and continued his address.

"I submit that the removal of Great Britain's representative from this Council was ill-considered. Ours was a founding nation, a permanent member, one with those which rebuilt the world after the Second World War. You can no more run us out of the Security Council as you can remove any other of the permanent members. Permanent means 'permanent'.

"Britain has done as much, or more, for the United Nations as any other. We helped conceive it, give birth to it, rear it to maturity, contributed money and arms to its causes – and finally we were thrown out.

"Consider where this could lead. Your refusal to recognise my father's government has a logical conclusion: enmity. One which the United Nations was brought about to prevent. Peace, universal understanding, mutual respect between nations and cultures, removal of barriers – these are the things for which this gathering of the nations was founded, the ideals for which it has striven, the goals which only can be considered the measures of its success or failure.

"We understand this Council sees the New Order as a different nation to the one which existed previously. But could not the same be said for each change from a Labour government to a Conservative one? Could it not be said of Russia, which is clearly no longer the same nation as when this organisation was founded? Merely due to the fact that there has been a change of government, it does not follow that it is not the same country. Britain is still Britain. Most of what was true of it a year ago is still so now. And since when was permanent membership conditional on continuity of regime?"

Throughout the Prince's speech, while every delegate was hanging on his every word, one exception, a gentleman sitting immediately behind the French representative, was looking at his tablet, reading messages and typing replies.

<But most of this Council regret having barred the UK>, the Frenchman typed in English. <My representative and most of the others mean to allow them back in.>

The response appeared on his screen. <Can you truly consider condoning an absolute monarchy, remembering

what France suffered two centuries ago to remove theirs. It must not be allowed to happen.>

<This council are more or less convinced that King Alfred's is a benevolent monarchy. More benevolent perhaps than many of the "democratic" governments represented here.> The French delegate touched "send".

In a moment words appeared on the screen. <The principle is too dangerous to be allowed to come to fruition.>

The delegate typed more. <Perhaps, but my representative cannot do this alone. He requires support.>

<Give me a moment.>

The delegate waited, dividing his gaze between the Prince and his tablet.

"In any case, the government has always belonged to my father. He has only ever allowed it to govern on sufferance. The United Kingdom is, in name and in fact, a kingdom. To quote every one of the King's speeches to Parliament: 'This year, my government will…' etcetera, etcetera. The difference now is that he operates directly. We are the same nation we have always been, but with stronger and more personal leadership.

"I urge… no, require, this Council to reinstate the United Kingdom's status and representative, effective immediately. My country unequivocally insists upon its rightful place here at the Security Council. This 'lockout' has been intolerable."

<While I support you personally,> the anonymous messenger typed, <I cannot immediately do so publicly. But you will have 'his' support.>

<Whose?> the French delegate typed and sent.

<Don't you know?>

The Frenchman touched his bottom lip with his fingertip, steadied his breathing, and typed. <One moment.>

He leaned forward, touching the French representative on the shoulder. A brief conference between them transpired, and the delegate showed the representative the conversation displayed on the screen.

The two men nodded to one another and resumed their previous attitudes.

<Very well. We will do our part.>

Finished speaking, the Prince leaned back and assumed a relaxed posture.

One of his aides leaned forward. "Excellent speech, Your Highness," he whispered.

"Nonsense," the Prince whispered sharply, mopping his brow with a handkerchief. "Not so much as a single clap."

"That's to be expected. They can't show their inclinations, in case they're in the minority. It's politics."

"Hmm." The Prince waited in silence as the Under-Secretary resumed the proceedings.

Archbishop Youngblood sat in front of his desktop computer. The opulent comfort of his office in Lambeth Palace rivalled that of the King's, an old-world ambience betrayed only by the modern personal computer into which he now peered.

He typed into an instant messenger application. <I trust you will. Our mutual friend will be most pleased. Signing off.>

While saving the chat transcript in an encrypted folder, he spoke to the speakerphone on his desk. "Are you still there, your Holiness?"

"Yes," came a European voice from the device, "I am here. Is it done?"

"It entirely depends now on who is the better orator. While I am grateful for your help, I trust you are not under the impression that the English church will return to Rome, your Holiness."

"Not all at once my friend, but is that not the direction your Church of England has been heading for a number of years now?"

***

The French representative addressed the Security Council.

"Great Britain, our great ally through the conflicts of two World Wars, and the whole of twentieth century history, continues to have a special place in the hearts of the French people, so we do not say this with pleasure, nor with anger at Britain or her people. But she, the United Kingdom as a national entity, has turned away from the democratic principles that make life in our modern world possible. Principles for which France – as well as the United States, and all former colonial peoples – shed their blood. The cost of democracy to each of our nations has been unbearably high. And Britain had led the way. When the power of the King was limited, back in the seventeenth century, she began a trend of democracy which spread and became what we call today 'the free world'.

"Which is why it would be wrong to accept her now as a fully-fledged absolute monarchy. It is little more than dictatorship. The free world has no room for such an abomination. Perhaps King Alfred's reign is benevolent. But it would require only his heir to change the situation completely – my apologies Your Highness for using you as a hypothetical example. It could as easily be one of your children, or one of theirs. A return to mediaeval ways is in keeping with neither a modern Europe nor a modern world. For the good of all, Britain can not be allowed to return to the Security Council."

The French representative's speech continued, taking different paths and employing different tactics. Before he had finished, the Security Council might as well have been baying for the Prince's blood.

One of the British consular staff leaned forward in his chair, speaking to the Prince over the clamour. "I've never seen them like this before. We had better get out before it turns even uglier."

The Prince surveyed the sea of hostile faces. He stood up, holding a hand out, drawing a breath and opening his mouth. He continued to observe the scene, as beads of sweat rapidly accumulated on his forehead, wetting his hair.

Noticing again the microphone, at desk level and well out of reach of his voice, Adrian sat down, leaned forward, and again drew in a breath and opened his mouth.

Adrian's eye caught that of the French representative, whose expression could have been either smugness or sympathy. The Prince continued looking at him until he realised his breath had gone and his mouth closed of their own accord. He attempted again to speak, again found himself unable.

The many men in the room were arguing among themselves or looking daggers at the Prince while shouting things he could not hear over the deafening murmur. The women were sitting quietly, perhaps waiting for the noise to die down, although among the delegates and representatives they were too few to make an impression.

The Prince stood up. He looked in the direction of the exit, and began to move. His four-man entourage quickly joined him, arranging themselves to hedge him on all sides as they made their way out.

As he moved, the Prince felt increasingly dizzy and breathless. Though for the most part no-one was touching him, the crowd was very vocal, very agitated, very visible, very close. He began to sway a little near the exit.

But it was only a moment before he was out of the council chamber and through the security screening area. Another few steps and he was through the door. Sucking in the warm New York air and feasting his eyes on the sunshine, the Prince had no time for relief before he was again surrounded by a press of bodies. United Nations security men crowded around him, augmented by a number of NYPD officers, all of whom helped to funnel him to his waiting limousine. At one point he thought he felt an open hand smack him on the back of his head as he was being hustled into the car.

Safely ensconced in his vehicle, the Prince was driven through the gates of the UN compound and onto the New York streets. He rolled down the window nearest him.

"Your Highness, please put the window up. We're not secure here."

"Just for a minute. I need the air."

And then he became aware of the crowd outside the limousine. Reporters, journalists, people with cameras and – a microphone, held in the hand of a lovely but aggressive television broadcaster impinged upon his personal space even inside the car.

"Your Highness, will you be staying in New York to enjoy the city at all? Which will be your hotel? I would love to have you in my studio," the woman said while, next to her, a television camera pointed itself at him.

"Tempting, but I'm afraid not. I'm needed back in Britain urgently." He flicked a button in the door, closing the window. The woman managed to extract her hand, but not the microphone, which the window held fast as the driver found an opening and sped away, the cable whipping away from the woman's handheld recording device.

Returning to his ship the Prince walked rapidly to his quarters, ignoring the salutes of any and all officers and ratings who greeted him along the way.

Stripping off his navy suit and leaving it on the floor, the Prince took a quick shower. Upon finishing he donned his dressing gown before using the ship's intercom system to locate Commander Indrani. "Jasmina," the Prince said, blotting his wet hair with the towel draped over his shoulder, "would you be so kind as to come to my quarters? And bring along a ration of the best grog. See you soon." Adrian had only minutes to wait, jiggling his foot or tapping something with his fingers and frequently looking at his watch all the while.

Soon, there was a knock on the door. Still clad in his dressing gown, he opened it. Commander Indrani stood in the corridor, immaculate in her uniform as always.

"Come in Jasmina."

She offered him a crystal decanter filled with light brown liquid. "Your grog, sir."

He took it from her. "Sit down my dear." Adrian found two crystal glasses, set them on the coffee table along with the decanter, and sat down next to her on the sofa.

"What can I do for you sir?"

"Well, I can think of many things." The Prince put a finger on her knee, stroking it lightly. "And I'm certain you know what they are." Taking his hand away from her person, he poured a small amount of liquor into each of their glasses. He pushed one toward her.

"Please sir, I know you may think–"

"You're so young, so beautifully exotic, so perfect. I can't stop thinking about you. Dreaming of you."

She pushed the drink back toward him. "First of all, not that you've ever asked me, but I don't drink. I've seen far too much of what this stuff can do to people, and I want no part of it."

Adrian took his glass and downed the contents in one swallow.

"Secondly sir, since you also never asked, I'm married." She held up her hand to show her wedding ring. "Happily. Three years now. I may be young, but I'm not a bimbo. I will not do what you're asking."

"Not even," he said, looking up at her while inclining his head downward, "if it's good for your career?"

"Not even," she said, inclining her head slightly upward, "if it destroys my career."

He exhaled deeply and leaned back, relaxing. "Very well, let's get to know each other a little better. What is your religion? Muslim?"

Indrani shook her head. "Christian."

"Really? So am I. In fact, as you may have heard, my father is head of the Christian church. And one day, I will be too."

She took a deep breath, heaved a heavy sigh. "The fact that you can even say that is proof enough that it can't be true. If you understood at all what the Church really is, you'd also understand that no man can be the head of it."

"Very well, Commander. That will be all. You may return to your duties."

Silenced, she looked at the floor as she stood up, turning toward the door. "Sir," she said, turning back to him, "I know you called me here because you're frustrated and angry and wanted some comfort, and I suppose I am flattered that you chose me above all the other women on this ship, but you can't find joy or peace that way. You can only find them in Christ – and He's the head of the Church."

He looked away from her. "Yes, thank you Commander. Now return to your duties."

"Sir, this is my duty – as a servant of God. If you trust in the Lord," she said, her voice uneven and her hands trembling almost imperceptibly, "with repentance and humility, then he will save you. It doesn't help or hinder that you're a prince. God is no respecter of persons."

"Jasmina, do you honestly think you're the first person who ever said that to me?"

"I don't know sir. But what if I'm the last?" She took a deep breath, quivering, hesitating. "Jesus Christ died on the cross to save his people. That could be you, Your Highness. John Newton once said, 'I am a great sinner, but Christ is a great saviour.'"

"Enough!" the Prince shouted. "I said, you may now return to your shipboard duties, Commander! That is an order!"

"Yes sir." She stood up and went to the door. "Is my career destroyed, Your Highness?"

"We'll see." He took the drink he had poured for her and drank it, closing his eyes.

Indrani left.

The Dominance sailed from New York without the Prince or his crew spending any time enjoying the city's many delights.

The first few days of the journey were uneventful, which gave Adrian time to drink, sulk, and ignore the running of the ship, safe in the knowledge there was another captain at hand.

Lonely and bored, there were several people he could, and did, phone to vent his dejection upon. On this occasion he phoned his wife.

"And what does your heart tell you, Adrian?"

"I don't know, Lillian," the Prince said. He sat at his desk in his quarters, doodling with a fountain pen on a hardcopy of an official communication from his father. "My mind tells me that on the one hand, I've failed you and the children. On the other hand, I've failed Father and the country. What does my heart tell me? I think it lies to me."

"The reason your heart is silent about your relationships – with me, the children, your father, and anyone else – is that you don't have one." Princess Lillian's voice quivered and quaked. "You have no heart Adrian. That is the only reason you can do the things that you do. Honestly, I don't know why you even called me instead of one of your bimbos. How about that latest one? The one who wears a boiler suit when she visits the Palace? Her false moustache is very convincing. Oh yes, I know all about her. So talk to her, or perhaps you can recruit some of the poor naive young girls serving on that ship of yours."

The Prince was visibly on the verge of tears, but somehow – whether by clenching his teeth, breathing deeply, or some unknown discipline – he did not let it come across in his voice. "Honestly, I also don't know why I called you. I pour out my heart and soul to you, and what do I get for it?"

"I told you Adrian, you don't have a heart. But I certainly hope you have a soul, so it can burn in hell."

The line went dead.

"Oh, woman!" He invoked the word as if it were a curse or an expletive. "What did I ever see in you? If I could go back in time, you'd be one of the first things I'd eliminate. I loved you! I truly did! Or, at least, I thought I did." He continued that way for some time, continuing to address the dead phone line and empty air in his quarters, cursing his wife, and everything to do with her.

He slid out of his chair and onto the floor, face wet with tears, his body wracked by convulsions and sobs.

***

The following day, he put on a uniform and went to the temporary officers' mess for his breakfast. He politely answered questions as to his health and well-being dishonestly, and otherwise sat in silence.

Afterward, he placed another call to London, this time to his own private detective, who was also following the Prince's current girlfriend, though with a different purpose. This detective's job was to report to the Prince the young woman's whereabouts and activities as they might pertain to her faithfulness. So far nothing had come to light. It seemed that the girl was fiercely loyal to her Prince. And with good reason: as long as she was his mistress she would be well cared and provided for.

Having received a good report of her, he said goodbye to the detective, and placed a call to the young woman herself.

She was young and beautiful, but also intelligent, holding down a good job at the Palace, which was how she had come to be in the Prince's orbit. Adrian had to try her several times before succeeding in reaching her on the telephone. So far his relationship with her had not been discovered by the media. Their carefulness in meeting unobserved had so far paid dividends, and for those who knew about their relationship – such as Lillian – it would not have been in their interest to inform the press.

Having asked for her in a disguised voice, which was easy for him because impressions were his best party piece, he reverted to normal once she was on the phone.

The Prince, addressing her as "darling", told her about the lack of sympathy he had received from his wife.

"My poor Prince," she said, sounding completely natural while laying on the sympathy thickly. "How good those bullies at the UN be so nasty to you?"

"You know how. You've seen it on the news, just like everyone else in the world. There is no way they can justify this." The Prince hung his head as he spoke.

"Well, not exactly 'no way'," she said with a pause for thought. "I mean, you can understand the Security Council being a bit... dubious... of any country leaving behind the democratic process."

"You're defending them?" The Prince sounded incredulous, even angry. "I thought you'd be on my side!"

"I am on your side, handsome. I'm just trying to see both sides. There are reasons why they might resist your father and his New Order, but they shouldn't use these bullying tactics against you, and they should definitely have made you welcome. After all, their grievance isn't with you, is it?"

"No it isn't," the Prince said with smug vindication. "I am not my father. They should have taken notice of that fact."

"Of course they should. And if they knew you like I do, they would have been much, much" – Adrian was certain he heard her licking her lips – "more respectful. Just like I'll be next time I see you."

"Not too respectful I hope. At least now I've got something to look forward to."

"You certainly have," she said with a sultry flourish.

That evening he went to the officers' mess for dinner with, if not a spring then at least a cushion in his step.

Nevertheless he kept to himself, and his demeanour that night was dark, lonely, dejected. He continued the same for most of the next day when, in the afternoon, he placed a call to his boys, Joseph and Cameron. After Adrian himself, Joseph was heir to the throne, though only eight years old.

"So boys, how's school?"

"It's fine, Father," Joseph said. He always spoke first, acting as his younger brother's spokesman. "Mrs Williams gave me full marks on my report!"

"Very good."

"And I coloured in a map of the world today," Cameron said, allowing his eight-year-old enthusiasm to run free. "Mr Restal told us that you can do the whole thing with only four colours, without two countries next to each other ever being the same."

"And were you able to do it?"

"Of course I did Father. I'm clever. You told me so. Remember? Only…"

The Prince challenged his son. "Only what?"

"Well, I did have to try three times. But one of the boys in my class needed five tries!"

"You see? I was right. You are clever. Have you seen your mother?"

"Of course Father," Joseph said, his tinny voice compromised by the speaker phone and the satellite connection. "We live with her. We see her every day."

"Will we see you again soon Daddy? I mean," – Cameron corrected himself – "Father?"

"I don't know. I'm going to be at sea for a while longer, and then I've got urgent business in London. So, perhaps. But your mother's taking good care of you, isn't she?"

"I suppose so," Joseph said. "Or at least, she gets Mrs Potts to take good care of us."

"And how are the polo team doing?"

"I don't know Father. I'm not on the polo team. I'm not old enough."

"Er, no, but you will be. You should keep tabs on it."

There followed a little more stilted conversation before the Prince told his sons that he had to go and attend to some urgent ship's business.

He finished the call and took up his bottle of gin.

3

Destruction

Adrian had not been drinking for long when Captain Roberts came to visit him.

"Really Your Highness, this is not on."

"What isn't?" The Prince stood near his bed, facing away from the Captain.

"This whole moping and brooding in your cabin thing."

"If I choose to 'mope and brood' it's my own affair. In any case, I come to meals in the mess."

"And that's good, except that you mope and brood there as well. You need to get back into circulation. Make your presence known aboard ship."

The Prince flopped heavily into his bunk. "I know, Dickie, I know."

Captain Roberts sat down and began picking up and handling the items on the desk. He examined a silver and gold sword letter opener, then a rough stone paperweight with a smooth engraved side. There were not many items to examine, and he stood up. "Come on. Get dressed, leave this room, and circulate. Give some orders. Tell the men to swab the decks or something."

Adrian covered his face with his hands. "It's not for you to give me orders."

"But it is for me," Roberts said, "to report to your father. What am I going to tell him?"

"Tell him whatever you want. I'm staying right here. How can I give any orders, how can I have any authority, after what happened in New York?"

"Forget about New York. Disregard it. Obviously the UN were never going to obey your orders. But the crew of this ship will. Your authority here is still intact. For now, at least."

"Just show myself? Just give some orders? That isn't going to change anything."

"Of course it will. That's how command works, you know that. You show yourself. You give some orders. Your presence, your reliability – you work yourself into their hearts and minds. It doesn't matter what you're feeling like inside. Do you think my crew know the real me? If they did they wouldn't follow me anywhere. It's a piece of theatre, something you put on, however you're feeling inside. Now, your ship needs you to be visible and in charge, for the sake of morale. You're the commanding officer on this ship, and your black mood affects the entire crew – myself included."

"All right," the Prince breathed. "Very well. I'll try. I'll try to put on the act you're describing. Will that make you happy? Then you can tell that to my father. Tell him I'm putting on an act, and everything is all right. But don't think I can just forget the UN."

"Fair enough. But you can at least think about it differently. You weren't defeated at the UN. It defeated itself. It is a self-defeating organisation."

"Whatever the UN is, it is not a school sports day. Everyone is not a winner. I lost. And therefore, Britain lost. Spin that when they begin imposing sanctions upon us."

"It won't come to that. You'll see."

"Fine. Not another word. I'll get dressed, come up to the bridge, put on my bravest face, and give a few orders. Maybe commend one, and rebuke another. That should make everything hunky-dory, yes?"

"It'll be a good start, Your Highness." The Captain saluted the Prince, and left.

Adrian turned to lay on his side, and squeezed his eyes shut. Nevertheless, tears escaped and ran on to his pillow.

In time, the Prince was as good as his word, emerging from his quarters showered and uniformed. Not only did he spend time on the bridge and issue orders, but also made himself available and approachable to those around him. He even toured the ship with some other officers, including

Commander Indrani, conducting spot inspections in the engine room, the ammunition magazine, and other areas. For the remaining days of the journey home he maintained the public attitude of an unflappable commanding officer.

Colonel Broadley enjoyed his new temporary HQ. Lt McGougan had ordered him to choose a place to use as a base of operations within the city of York.

Though the enemy had been routed from the cathedral, the damage the historic building had sustained left it wide open to the weather, as well as unsafe. The stones that still occasionally fell within its from its weakened fabric were large enough and heavy enough to destroy both a hardhat and the person wearing it, so the Minster was off-limits for the time being.

Broadley was never even required to justify his eventual choice of the Jorvik Viking Centre, a popular tourist attraction which showed visitors a slice of life in a viking settlement. McGougan accepted it, approved it, and then left town, leaving Broadley to command the troops as they continued the work of liberating the city of York from the militia.

By now the city centre was almost entirely under the control of the army. All civilians not involved in the conflict – meaning those who had not joined the militia – had been successfully evacuated. All buildings in the city centre were being systematically combed for remaining insurgents, and the process was nearly complete. A new police force was being recruited, and many of those new recruits were already on the streets, keeping peace in the city while the Army continued to clear it. More police continued to be added to their ranks, as Army intelligence officers and psychologists cleared those veteran personnel who had never been affiliated with AS-ONE.

"Good afternoon Lieutenant," Col Broadley said, saluting his superior officer. "When did you get back in town, sir?"

"Only in the last few minutes. I like what you've done with the place, Major." McGougan glanced right and left at the crooked primitive huts with roughly thatched roofs, set on a simulated road which appeared to be straw and mud. They were elements in an atmospheric re-creation of a Viking settlement, albeit scaled down to fit inside the indoor area. The ceiling was painted to simulate an evening sky, and moody lighting created an old world atmosphere.

"Not that I'm criticising, mind you," McGougan said, "but why did you choose the Jorvik for your HQ?"

"I've always enjoyed visiting this place with the wife and kids, and I often said how I'd like to spend more time here. Well, now I can. I mean, don't you love the atmosphere sir?"

"Hmm."

"In any case, it's better than the other location I was thinking about."

"And what was that?"

"Clifford's Tower. The facilities here are much better, don't you think?"

"As I said, 'hmm'. Now, let's change the subject. General Montgomery is very keen that we should get the conservators in to begin assessing the Minster with a view toward repairs. Funny, given that he was the one who ordered us to blow it up, but never mind. 'Orders is orders.'"

"Very good sir. I reckon it'll be two more days before we can be sure there'll be no further enemy activity."

"Fine. Then carry on Colonel. Oh yes, and His Majesty sends his compliments."

"Thank you sir."

The Lieutenant departed, leaving Broadley to his own devices again, which consisted of organising, delegating, and, occasionally, getting his own hands dirty. Today it would be joining his men in sweeping another building or two before getting down to some paperwork.

Prince Adrian stood in the doorway of the situation room. "Good morning, Father."

King Alfred looked from the map to his son. "Ah, son, what tidings from New York?" He walked toward the Prince.

Lindsey, who had been standing at the King's shoulder with his notebook open, stayed still.

"Well, I'm afraid no good has come out of New York, Father," Adrian said. A uniformed soldier muttered an apology as he squeezed past the Prince. "No, it's not really New York, is it? It's the United Nations. And they are just as intractable as the Scots. Worse perhaps."

Alfred put his hand on Adrian's arm and guided him into the corridor, walking with him. "You're not letting it get to you this time, are you?"

"I–" the Prince's words choked on empty air. He cleared his throat. "I'm much better now." He paused, took a deep breath, and cleared his throat again. "I'm definitely much better now."

"Tell me all about it," the King said as they passed two men in suits walking the opposite direction.

Following at a respectful distance, Lindsey also dodged the suited men.

"Well, you may recall I was none too keen to go. But you so wanted me to that I decided to make the best of it. And the sailing to New York was very good. Lunch with the ratings, dinner with the officers – it was simply good times, good food, camaraderie. But then we arrived in New York, and everything changed. A cold reception. But when I gave my speech at the Security Council they seemed attentive and sympathetic enough, until the French representative spoke. And I must say, I now understand first-hand why we spent all those centuries at war with the French. At any rate, I suppose you know the rest. Then I went back to the ship and we left. Six days to get there for six hours in New York. A bit of a wasted trip."

"It was a gamble," the King said, "which didn't pay." They turned into the Garden Room, its gaping hole closed with a large thick plastic sheet which undulated as the breeze filtered past it from outside. He waved to the plasterers and bricklayers who were busily working. "Would you lads leave us alone for a little while? Take a cup of tea or something."

The men acknowledged and left the room, while Lindsey moved into an inconspicuous corner and continued taking notes.

"Well, in any case," Adrian continued, "we set off back. And for the first few days I was really not myself. But the crew brought me round, especially Captain Roberts and Commander Indrani. The Captain helped me to see it wasn't my fault. The problem lay with the UN, not with me. Once I realised that, everything was much easier. I was able to relax and enjoy the trip home, without having to think about" – the Prince's brow began to quiver, and his bottom lip followed suit – "about what a hopeless and utter failure I am." Adrian gave in to deep sobs. He turned to his father and rested his head on the older man's shoulder, reaching up to him with his hands in a tentative embrace. "That beastly Security Council, I thought they were going to stone me – with their staplers, mobile phones, anything."

As the Prince continued choking his words out between sobs, King Alfred put a hesitant arm around his son, patting him uncertainly on the back.

"I thought I was drowning in that horrible room, people all around me baying for my blood, waving papers, shouting. Then they hustled me outside like a naughty schoolboy and the policemen, crowding all around me, moving me along until I stumbled over their feet. And that horrible reporter pummelling me with questions in my weakest moment." Adrian took a step back from his father, even as his face was wet with tears. "Is that what it is to be King? Then don't ever die, Father, because I don't want it."

"I–" Alfred let his hands drop to his sides, then clasped them behind him. His brow furrowed and his eyes darkened. "I'm not going to live forever son. Therefore, the throne is your destiny. It's not always as you describe it. It can be the making of a man. It's unfortunate there can only be one, but one day it's going to be you. So make yourself ready. Learn how to cope with hardships and disappointments. You'll have those, aplenty. But you'll also have successes. Triumphs.

So make yourself ready, boy. You're fifty now, aren't you? You've done everything too late. You married too late, had children too late, and now you've tasted power too late. It's more difficult to get accustomed to it at your age. Even more so at mine. But I have, and you will. You will learn the ways of power. You will be King. There's no avoiding it." He clapped his son on the shoulder. "All right?"

Adrian wiped his tears away with a handkerchief, which he stuffed in his pocket. "Yes Father," he said, his voice flat and steady. "I'm sorry for being such a disappointment. I'll do my best. Of course you're right. It's my destiny. I need to stop moaning about it and embrace it. I'll make you proud. You'll see." He brought his hands together in front of him with a clap, holding them there for a moment. "Well, I've got a few things left to do in town, and then I'll get back to my ship. With your permission Father?"

"It really will be all right, son. We've almost got Britain back to normal. Most of the AS-ONE people have been rounded up, and we have loyal police back on the streets, as well as in the Palace."

"That's good, Father. I'm glad to hear it. Now, with your leave, I'll be on my way and about my business."

"Of course son. Don't forget to see your sister while you're in town."

"I won't. Thank you Father."

Adrian left the room, wiping his eyes, while the King looked tiredly at Lindsey, who completed his writing and closed the book.

Princess Frances was hard at work in one of the smaller dining rooms of Kensington Palace. Papers were arranged all over the neoclassical dining table large enough to seat twelve people. She had taken to working in this room after finding that she could not keep these papers organised on the relatively small desk in her office. They were organised into neat stacks organised in a grid fashion with approximately one-centimetre spaces between each stack.

On her own insistence her father had entrusted her with checking over the papers that came and went to and from his possession. They had decided it would be prudent to keep another family eye on the various bills and documents with attention toward any content that might adversely affect either the Royal family or the New Order. Some MPs, in drafting bills, would hope either to give themselves more power or the Royals less, while others made more honest mistakes which reflected on their difficulty in adapting to the new ways.

Princess Frances, wearing a pair of reading glasses, was poring over one of the papers, when Adrian entered.

She continued staring down at the paper.

The Prince stood, quietly waiting, until it seemed that his sister might never notice him. He cleared his throat quietly.

Looking up at him, she smiled and rose, went over to him and embraced him. "I'm so sorry Adrian," she said as she held him. "How long have you been standing there?"

"Sorry? For what?"

She released him from her embrace, backing up enough to look at him. "For New York, of course." Her brow furrowed. "The Security Council."

Adrian waved a hand. "Pish-posh. Water under the bridge."

Frances took another step back, frowning. "Oh. I must say I'm surprised to see you taking it so well. Father must be impressed."

"Er, well, I did rather… lose it… in front of him."

"I see," Frances said with a nod. "And what did Father say?"

The Prince inhaled. "He told me to 'man up', basically."

The Princess raised an eyebrow, half-smiling. "Sensitive of him."

"No, he's right. And I am manning up."

"But–" The Princess looked at him, searching his eyes. "Fine. Do that. But don't let Father make you forget who you are."

Adrian gave Frances a slight smile. "Don't worry. I know who I am."

"All right," the Princess said slowly. "So, how long are you in town?"

"Only until tomorrow."

"And what will you be doing? Will you have time to take dinner with me tonight?"

"No. I'm sorry, but I've got errands to run, and I'm quite tired."

"Very well," the Princess said. "Perhaps another time."

"Perhaps," the Prince said. Again the slight smile.

"And what will you do tomorrow? Go back to your ship?"

"And wait for orders, yes."

Her eyebrows clenched as she tightened her lips and shook her head. "There's definitely something different about you. Waiting for orders, patient, calm… you've even dropped your usual sarcasm."

"Yes, well, getting shot down in both the Scottish Parliament and the United Nations Security Council does that to a man." A fleeting look of worry or sadness passed over Adrian's face.

She touched his arm. "Oh, but I thought your speech at the UN was… fantastic. In fact, I thought the Security Council were going to apologise to you. I was shocked by things that Frenchman said – we all were – and how the rest responded to him. Everyone – my staff here, and Father's at Buck House – we all watched, and we were behind you all the way. You acquitted yourself brilliantly. You have nothing to be ashamed of."

The Prince looked to one side, and then at his finger-nails. "Oh, I've got a few things."

"Well," she said, taking him in her arms and hugging him, "I've never been so proud of you. Father and I both love you. You know that, don't you?"

He extricated himself from her embrace then turned away from her, looking at the floor. "Yes. Of course I know it.

You said it, so I believe you. All the years we've spent fighting and refusing to speak to each other notwithstanding – it's all about right now, isn't it?"

"Yes it is, as a matter of fact," she said, looking at the back of his head. It's water under the bridge, as you said. Now please stay for dinner."

"No, I really must be going."

The Prince left Kensington Palace for his own residence of Clarence House. He found his a woman waiting there for him.

"Since you weren't here I didn't have to come in in my boiler suit. I just entered with the staff. The guards on the door even fixed me up with a lanyard. See?"

The Prince afforded her a little smile. "Hmm. Credibility. It's a many-splendoured thing."

"Credibility, eh? I'm not going to have that any time soon, am I? Not while you're still married to Her Royal Highness."

"Don't worry, Olivia. I won't be married to her for much longer."

"Good." They entered his office, and as she closed the door behind them she took his hand and pulled him close for a long kiss.

The Prince broke away from her, taking his seat behind the desk.

"In the meantime," she said, "I've got a job here. I'm your new stenographer."

"I didn't know I needed a stenographer."

"Oh, you need a stenographer all right," she said as she sat down in one of the chairs in front of the desk. "It's absolutely essential." She made ready her pen and steno pad. "In fact, we should get started right away. Now, Your Highness, dictate to me. Be… my… dictator." She pursed her lips and looked at him over the top of her glasses.

Adrian breathed a weary sigh. "As… alluring as you make it sound, I haven't got any dictation for you today. I've been told my children are coming over soon."

"The young princes, eh? Well, I suppose that's all right. I mean, you don't see them that often, do you? I'll get out of your way then. But if you need to perform any dictation afterward…"

The Prince stood up with her. "Definitely. After all, I've only got tonight, as I'll be back on my ship tomorrow."

She stamped her foot lightly in a show of mock vexation, and in an endearingly pouty whine she said, "How come I hardly ever see you any more?"

"Needs must, my dear. I'll see you tonight."

"Would you mind if I stayed long enough to say hello to the little princes?"

"No, I don't suppose so. In fact, you might as well have afternoon tea with us. I must warn you, however, we usually have pizza for afternoon tea when the boys come over."

"Pizza?" She feigned indignation. "In a Royal residence? What impropriety! Ah well, as you say, needs must."

Soon the children arrived, transported by bodyguards and chauffeur until they were left in the Prince's presence. He introduced them to Miss Trafford, his stenographer, who, he explained, wanted to meet them.

"Are you Father's mistress?" the older prince asked.

Her face went red as she gasped, speechless.

Adrian looked uncertainly between his son and Miss Trafford. "Where did you hear such a thing, Joseph?"

"From mother."

"Well, when a woman has servants, they refer to her as 'Mistress'. Perhaps mother was making a joke." Adrian clasped his hands behind his back and smiled at his son.

"What's a stenographer?" the younger prince asked, stumbling over the long word several times before saying it correctly.

"That's a good question, Cameron," Adrian said. "She's someone who helps Father in all sorts of ways."

"Your father dictates letters to me," Miss Trafford said, "and I write them down as he speaks them, in a language called shorthand, which is English but you wouldn't be able to read it."

The children required a demonstration, and Trafford obliged. They were entranced by the seemingly meaningless scribbles that she produced, and intrigued by her assurances that she would be able to read it all back later in order to type it.

They took a walk together in the formal gardens, the boys enjoying hiding behind things and jumping out to frighten their father, who made a half-hearted pretence at being scared.

Being children, the young princes moved from activity to activity, while finding themselves bored with the Prince's lack of insight as to what will keep the young boys' attention. Miss Trafford proved more successful in that regard.

Soon it was time for afternoon tea, and – as good as his word – several boxed pizzas were waiting for them in the Prince's dining room, spreading their tempting aroma within a generous radius.

The young princes watched their father eat what was, to him, a strange and uncomfortable meal. The boys and Miss Trafford picked up and ate the slices of pizza with their hands, while Adrian used a knife and fork.

But their father smiled at them, spent time with them, ate with them, and left them feeling it had been perhaps the nicest, most relaxed time they had spent with him in quite a while.

After the boys had gone back to their mother, the Prince spent the rest of the night in the company and the arms of Olivia Trafford.

Likewise, she could not have remembered a time when the Prince was kinder to her and gave her more tender attention than he did that night.

Prince Adrian rose early in the morning, donned his captain's uniform, gave his mistress a kiss as she slept, and was driven away in his waiting Rolls-Royce limousine.

With a small police escort the limousine quietly returned him to his ship at Portsmouth. Flanked by his bodyguards as far as the ship's gangway, their responsibility for him ended as, not being naval personnel, they were not allowed on board.

"Permission to come aboard?"

"Granted, Your Highness," said the young officer whose task it was to greet the ship's senior captain.

Walking along the corridors as he made his way to the bridge, Adrian was saluted by the passing multitude of ratings and officers. He returned each and every salute with equal decorum and courtesy, greeting as many as he knew personally by name.

"Captain on the bridge!"

The Prince did not see who had spoken, though he recognised the voice. Those who were not already standing stood to attention.

"At ease, men," he said, glancing at and making eye contact with Commander Indrani. "As of this moment, we haven't got any orders. But that could change at any time. So, for the moment we will patrol the coast and concentrate on keeping the ship shipshape and Bristol fashion." He looked around the bridge, catching the eyes of several of the officers and crew. "Carry on."

Captain Roberts came over to the Prince and spoke to him in a low voice, not hushed, but not so the others would hear. "And how are you, Your Highness? Shipshape?"

The Prince stared at the floor for a moment, before looking into the eyes of the Captain. "I'm ready," he said as he paused for a weary breath, "to set sail. So let's get out to sea. We are sailors, after all."

"So we are, Your Highness," Roberts said. "You heard the Captain, people! To sea! Let's keep these waters safe, from… whatever." He smiled at the Prince, who looked back at him with a pleasant and polite demeanour.

The two Captains each took up a pair of binoculars and began to scan the horizon of the English Channel.

"Well," the Captain said as he gazed through the lenses, "I don't see any pirates."

The Prince also continued scanning. "Nor any Scots, nor UN delegates."

Captain Roberts smiled and laughed as he let the binoculars down from his eyes. "Ha! That's more like it, Your Highness."

"Carry on Dickie." The Prince put down his binoculars. "I'll be in my quarters."

As the Prince made for the exit, Commander Indrani approached him. "I haven't got any particular duties right now. Could I could bring you a tray of tea?"

He glanced from right to left, and spoke quietly. "Only tea?"

"And conversation perhaps. If you're agreeable to that."

Looking into her eyes intently, he stepped forward slightly so he was standing as close to her as shipboard propriety would allow. "I think not Commander. I want to be alone for a while."

"Oh. As you wish sir." She saluted him and returned to her duties.

Standing at the door, the Prince looked at the various crew members on the bridge, registering each face, each body, and their various actions. Two were looking at a map, one was talking to someone in another part of the ship via internal communications, one was bringing Captain Roberts something to sign, another was interacting with a radar screen.

The Prince turned and walked through the door. Commander Indrani looked up from her station to see the Prince go, a frown on her lips and a furrow in her brow.

Corporal Flavel's team stacked up at the front and back doors of the five-storey insurance brokerage building near central York. The two halves of the team kept in touch by radio, counting down to the moment they would breach, enter, and clear the building one floor at a time.

Intelligence had been obtained of this and two similar buildings which have been harbouring a large number of remaining insurgents, and subsequent observations appeared to support this.

Even now, two other teams were positioned to enter the other two buildings. The three teams coordinated their efforts, preparing to take the three sites simultaneously, giving no opportunity for one group of insurgents to warn the others that a strike was imminent.

The teams worked under cover of night in full camouflage. They were covered by observers in adjacent buildings using medium-range night-vision optics, watching the windows of the target buildings for signs of life. So far, the coast appeared to be clear. The lack of enemy activity inside the buildings pointed to the possibility that the insurgents were asleep, if they were actually there at all. The lack of activity could equally have suggested that they had somehow known the army were coming and had fled. They had not been observed to have left, and the assumption was that they were still in the buildings.

Colonel Broadley himself was observing from a window directly opposite the premises Corporal Flavel's team were preparing to breach. The observers as well, including Broadley, had gone dark – lights off, camouflage on – and were ready with snipers to offer whatever support they could.

"All teams stacked up and ready Sir," the crackly voice of Corporal Flavel said through the Colonel's radio.

"Very well Corporal," Broadley responded. "I trust your judgement as to the best time to breach."

"No better time than the present, Sir. We're exposed out here."

The Colonel looked around at the men in the room who, ready with their rifles, gave him a thumbs-up. "Very well Corporal. Breach and clear."

The snipers made ready, each one covering particular windows and doors by prior agreement.

"On my mark, all teams breach and clear," Corporal Flavel said quietly into his radio. "Three, two, one, mark!"

Simultaneously on the doors of each of the three buildings, charges popped and flashed, causing small showers of wood and metal shards.

Where the doors hadn't fallen inward of their own accord, each team kicked them and entered.

As his team began to swarm in, Flavel saw near the floor a thin and brief shaft of red light in a wisp of dust, faint but visible.

"Lasers!" the Corporal shouted. "Everyone freeze!"

Too late.

Across the street, Colonel Broadley felt the heat of the red fireball which engulfed the building into which he had sent his men. The shockwave from the explosion shattered the windows, forcing shards, himself, and his snipers back with incandescent pressure against the room's internal walls. Colonel Broadley lost consciousness almost immediately as shards of glass bedded into his skin.

One of the other buildings exploded as well, whose team never saw it coming.

The third team, warned by the two explosions, proceeded with caution. Placing smoke grenades to reveal the lasers, they proceeded to avoid them. Entering the building, the team were impatient for blood in the light of the fate of the other teams. But corporal Longworth, reasoning that the other floors of the building may be rigged as well, pulled them out on the basis that they did not have enough time to sweep the entire site right now – not before they had attempted to rescue any survivors from the other two blasts.

Within a quarter of an hour, firemen were battling the blazes, a complete lack of survivors among the strike teams had been established, and the unexploded building was sealed off, under guard, and being swept of all traps as a matter of urgency.

Colonel Broadley was out on the street, sitting on a low wall next to an ambulance, its flashing lights bathing the scene in red and blue which complemented the glow of the fire. A medic was hunched over him, extracting the last fragment of glass from his face. None of the shards had breached his clothing, but his face and hands had received numerous injuries and were – to the casual observer – severely sunburnt.

Broadley grimaced, clenching his teeth as the shard was removed. The medic proceeded to apply topical antiseptic and painkiller to his face and hands. He let the man continue while he talked to Corporal Lulworth.

"Obviously they didn't blow themselves up," the Colonel said, "so where are they?"

"Don't know, sir," Lulworth said. "And it'll be awhile before we can investigate the explosion sites, even after the fires are out."

"That's why we'll have to focus our efforts on the one that didn't blow up. That's enough, doc." Broadley turned his face and brushed the medic's hand away as he stood up and headed toward the endangered building.

At that moment several cars exploded in rapid sequence and, for the second time that night, the colonel was thrown to the ground by the blast, along with a large number of other soldiers and policemen.

After he didn't know how many seconds, the Colonel got up. The windows of the ambulance, together with those of all the remaining cars and nearby buildings, were shattered, and the three cars were on fire with vigorous flames leaping up. The medics were already busy checking for injuries.

A manhole cover in the middle of the street was not properly fitted, having presumably been disturbed by the explosion.

Despite the topical pain relievers that had been applied to the Colonel's face, he could feel the effect of additional burns which showed on his face.

A young private emerged from around the corner at a run, saw the Colonel and approached him. "Sir, they've hit us all over the place. Exploding cars on every street. Some of 'em are ours, only just arrived, so they couldn't have been rigged earlier. They're here."

"We haven't seen anyone," the Colonel said. "Have you?"

"No sir. Me and the others thought for sure there weren't any of 'em left. Above ground at least."

Broadley looked again at the unsealed manhole cover. He snapped his fingers, wincing with the pain it caused, and pointed. "Maybe that's it. They're not above ground." He looked at the ground near himself and then to the spot where he had come to after the explosion. His walkie-talkie was still there, and he picked it up. He twisted the knobs, pressed the buttons, and hit it a couple times. "Dead. Private, find me a working radio. We have to take this fight underground."

HMS Dominance had an easy time on the calm waters of the English Channel. Its patrol of the English coastline was uneventful, but the crew were accustomed to such journeys. Though some would have preferred action, most were content with such times in which they could simply live the life of a sailor.

It was not so, however, for the Captain. The officers and crew were united with the Captain in their concern.

"This isn't right, even for him," Roberts said. "We've been underway for, what, a full day now. That's three meals without a sign of him. And just as he seemed to be doing so well."

Standing on an exposed raised platform just outside the bridge, they hunched in their greatcoats against the chill wind.

"I could tell something was wrong when he came on board yesterday. He was different." Indrani spoke loudly against the rush of the wind.

"You and your feminine intuition. I noticed something too, but I thought it was an improvement. More mature, less of a brat." He sliced the air in front of him horizontally with his hand. "Those comments are off the record mind you. I want you to take him a tray of tea, maybe some breakfast. Insist he speaks to you. Don't come back here until you've seen him."

"Yes sir."

Indrani made her way to the kitchens where she procured a silver trolley loaded with the ship's best china tea service. There was also a selection of things the Prince might like for breakfast. She ordered the cabin boy to push the trolley and accompany her to the Prince's quarters. They arrived at his door, and she knocked.

No answer.

She knocked again, louder.

Still no response.

"Your Highness! I need to speak with you, please!"

Still no response.

"What do we do?" the young seaman asked the Commander.

Indrani sighed. "We get an engineer down here to force this door open."

In a moment she was on the comms, finding someone who could help.

The engineer came and forced the door release, and it slid open a little.

Indrani slipped a hand through and began to push the door open. "Stay here."

She stepped into the Captain's quarters. The cabin boy, engineering, and several other crew members who had gathered with curiosity, waited.

They listened, each one straining his ears for the sound of Indrani's footsteps, swallowed up though they were by the continuous hum and thrum of the ship's systems.

A scream of horror sounded from within the Captain's suite.

It was Indrani. "No, no, no, no, please, no!"

Entering the suite for themselves, the gathered crew members saw what had so startled the Commander.

One end of the Prince's necktie was fastened to a solid overhead pipe in the bathroom. The other end was fastened just as securely to his neck, biting deeply. His feet were suspended a mere centimetre from the floor.

Indrani stood, a hand cupped over her mouth and tears running down her cheeks, looking at the Prince as his suspended body swung and spun ever so slightly with the air currents she had introduced by entering the room.

The others gasped or wept, and some dashed from the room in revulsion.

"Go tell the Captain what's happened," Indrani said, her voice constricted, looking at the junior officer next to her.

"I– I don't think I can ma'am. Could you do it please?" he said, holding back his own sobs and vomit. "You are the superior officer ma'am."

"Right," the Commander said, wiping the tears away from her cheeks with her open hands. "You arrange for him to be taken down and" – she paused as she fought down a wave of nausea – "laid on his bed. The rest of you – out! There will be no gawking." Indrani turned on her heels and left the room.

In a short time, the Captain arrived, as did the detachment from security. The Captain got on with the work leading the team who would take down the Prince's body and arrange it on the bed, working with a junior officer.

"I'm sorry sir, but as head of security I cannot allow the Prince'sbody to be moved. The scene mustn't be compromised until it's been photographed and examined."

"Steve," the Captain said through clenched teeth, "I will not allow His Highness – I mean, the body – to remain like this one moment longer. This is the Prince of Wales we're talking about, man."

The ship's medical officer and his assistants, at the Captain's nod, gathered around the Prince, three supporting the body while one began cutting the necktie with scissors. After snipping through half the thickness, the remainder snapped under the weight, and the medics carried the body horizontally, gently and with respect, setting it down on the bed. All backed away except for doctor, who, kneeling by the bed, checked for vital signs as a formality. But the coldness of the corpse's skin, and the stiffness of the limbs left no actual need to check for a heartbeat. The doctor closed the body's open eyes, but found his efforts to arrange the head and arms in a posture of repose frustrated by rigor mortis.

"Subject pronounced dead at ten o'clock," the doctor said, looking at his watch. "Time of death unknown, but likely between twenty-three-hundred and oh-six-hundred hours."

The most junior medic wrote notes.

"Give me those scissors," the doctor said, holding a hand out. "Taking them, he cut away the loop of necktie which still clung tightly to the body's neck and, standing up, handed it to the junior medic.

"I'm going to enter a protest," the head of security said to Captain Roberts. "The scene has been compromised and evidence removed."

"You protest all you like, son," Roberts said through his teeth. "That's your privilege and your duty. But spare a thought for how His Majesty would feel it if he could see what was happening in here. Leaving his son swinging on the gibbet wouldn't have him best pleased. Now clear and seal this room. Then you can commence your investigation."

The Captain departed.

"Alright ladies and gentlemen, you heard the Captain. Everyone out."

Of the dozen or so crew members crowded into the Captain's quarters, two crossed themselves, and all obediently left.

Commander Indrani, still standing in the corridor outside, continued to weep.

Captain Roberts wanted to tell the King the news himself, man-to-man, but he was required to observe the chain of command, and so it fell to Admiral Billington to inform the King that his son was dead.

Instead, Roberts took to the ship's loudspeaker system.

"Attention all crew members. This is the Captain speaking. Many of you will have heard the news by now through word-of-mouth, but I want you to hear it from me. Our senior captain, the Prince of Wales, to whom all of you have shown proper respect and deference, the son of His Majesty King Alfred, long may he reign, and my personal friend, is dead. He was found in his cabin this morning. Out of respect for His Majesty the King I will not comment further on the circumstances of the Prince's death, and I require that none of you do until the investigation is complete.

"For the short period he was with us on the HMS Dominance, we came to know him better as a man rather than as a royal personage looking out from the television screen or waving from his limousine. For my own part I shared meals and drinks with him, and for yours I know many of you did too. Let us remember him well, as the man of high estate who nevertheless took meals with the ratings at lunchtime, and with the officers for his dinner. The man who, despite his misgivings, bravely spoke to hostile assemblies, the first poor reception of which did not stop him from proceeding with the second. Where he made friends, let them be our friends. And where men came out as his enemies, let them be our enemies as well.

"Spare a thought or a prayer for His Majesty the King, who had pinned his hopes and dreams on the promise of his son, and who must now weep as a father. His Majesty will need our support as much as anyone.

"One more thing. Think not of the glimpses of the Prince's life which we've seen – whether up close or at a distance – as a piece of theatre, his ways often being extreme and perhaps out of the realms of what we might consider common sense. Rather, think of them as a piece of a man – a private man in the public eye – a piece which he allowed us to see. Which of us don't have our contradictions, our foibles, our lapses in common sense? A wise man once said, 'We like a man for his qualities, but we love him for his faults.'

"This afternoon the Padre will offer a short service of remembrance for His Highness Prince Adrian. He'll also be offering one-to-one counselling, to whoever might request it.

"The Union Jack flies at half-mast. That is all. Carry on."

The crew went about their remaining duties that day with heavy hearts, hands, and eyes.

"General Montgomery, Your Majesty," Lindsey said.

King Alfred sat at his desk, newspapers spread out on the surface, all open to the Prince's obituary. He did not look up from his reading, his face obscured by shadow as he hunched over the desk.

"Your Majesty," Montgomery said as he entered the room, "I am so sorry I couldn't get here sooner, but I'd like to offer my condolences in person."

"Go on then," Alfred said, voice flat, eyes on the newspapers.

The General looked around, acknowledging Lindsey before looking back to the King. "My… condolences…" he said, pausing again, "are given. Barbara also wished you to know the sadness she feels."

"You didn't want him in the army," the King said, eyes still down. "That was why he entered the navy. You didn't want him. He would have been better off with you." He stood up, looking at the General. His clothes were wrinkled, his tie loose, his face unshaven, his eyes darkly shadowed and narrow. "Effectively, you killed him."

His expression changing from sympathetic, to blank, to hurt, in the space of a second, the General took a deep, ragged breath. "Your Majesty, the army would have been proud to have His Highness among its number. I don't recall raising any objections. He preferred Naval service. That's all."

"You call me a liar then."

"No, Your Majesty. But you've been misinformed. As I said, my condolences are given. Is there anything I may do for you?"

"Only leave me to my grief." The King sat again, looking back to the newspapers.

"As you wish, Your Majesty. Please call me if there's anything you need."

The General hesitated, casting uncertain looks at Lindsey and the King, and left.

Many wished to visit the King that day. Only a few were granted access.

The next was Prime Minister Hollings. "Good afternoon, Your Majesty." Hollings stood gravely, his thin lips stretched in a purposeful but subtle frown.

The King said nothing, merely looking at his newspapers. He turned the page.

"Parliament are united in their grief for the Prince, and in sympathy for you," Hollings said.

"Are they indeed?" Alfred looked up at the Prime Minister, whose face registered surprise at the King's tired and drawn appearance. "Quincy, we both know how many of the current crop of Ministers of Parliament hold me in so little regard as could only be termed hatred. And you ask me to believe that they are united in grief? Don't insult my intelligence."

"You Majesty, that was the message Parliament wished to convey. I present it with no comments as to their honesty. But as for myself personally," Hollings said, frowning, "I am greatly grieved."

"You personally? Don't make me laugh," the King sneered. "To you, personally, my son sent letters asking you, and your farcical House of Commons, to consider certain issues near to his heart, or to point out some poll or research he thought would help you in your deliberations. You never respected him. You never took any of his suggestions seriously. You never implemented any of his ideas. Effectively, you killed him."

"Now Your Majesty," the visibly uncomfortable Prime Minister said, "that's hardly fair. I carefully read each of his letters. But what was I to do? Parliament is– was a democracy. We had to vote on things, take public opinion into account, and so on. What else could I have done?"

"You have brought me the sympathies of Parliament. Is there anything else? No? Then our weekly meeting is ended. Good day." The King sat back down, looking at his desk.

Hollings regarded the King for a moment, as if trying to look under his skin. "Then… good day, Your Majesty." He turned, and left.

"Blair, I won't see anyone else. Cancel everything."

"Everything Your Majesty? Until when?"

"Until further notice. Cancel them all." He crossed his arms, resting them on the desk, and rested his head on his arms, face down.

"Is that wise?" Blair spoke tentatively. "Surely the New Order must continue?"

"Wise?" Alfred raised his head, looking at Blair with a mad glint in his eye. "What do you know of wisdom? Do you not have an inside view into everything that happens in my family? Don't you serve the God who 'revealeth secrets'? Why did you not see this coming? Effectively, you killed my son." Alfred sighed, while Lindsey gaped at him. "Leave me. I shan't be requiring your services any longer."

"Your Majesty," Lindsey said, drawing a deep breath, "I'm no prophet. I can't foresee things like this, and I don't know exactly why God brings such trials. But if they bring you to the end of yourself, maybe you'll understand in your heart and bones that the only one you can rely on is Jesus Christ – and then they won't have come in vain. That said, I am truly sorry for your loss. I only knew the Prince a little, but I only would have ever wanted the best for him. Not I, nor anyone, would have wished this upon him. And I won't leave you, unless you actually give me the sack. Until you do, I'm here for you, even if only to take the minutes of your meetings and organise your diary."

The King looked back down in his papers. He turned away so that Lindsey couldn't see him, and rubbed the tears from his eyes. "Then get Captain Roberts on the phone. I wish to speak to him."

Lindsey went through the necessary steps of initiating a call to a naval ship at sea, and within a few minutes had raised Captain Roberts.

"Your Majesty! I'm so glad you called. Please accept my

. .

56 *Send Him Victorious*

most heartfelt condolences. His Highness had become a valued part of the crew, and we are all gutted. Is there anything we can do, sir?"

"Only one thing, Dickie. Tell me how you failed him so badly. You were meant to look after him! I put him directly in your care. You were meant to keep his hopes up, keep his dreams alive. Effectively, you killed him."

The line went silent for a moment, save for the Captain's breathing. "Your Majesty, I've been thinking about that a lot lately. I do feel responsible. I don't know what I could have done differently, but… I've lost crew members before, and I always feel responsible. I am sorry, Your Majesty. He was my friend, and I will miss him."

The line went silent for a moment.

"Let me know," the King said, "what your investigation brings to light."

"Of course, Your Majesty. But I hope you understand that nothing will come to light. This is a simple case of – I'm sorry to have to say it – suicide. The investigation is only to ascertain the exact circumstances."

King Alfred abruptly hung up the phone, stood up, and crossed the room.

Lindsey arose in surprise, moving ahead of the King to open the door for him as he walked rapidly through the corridors of Buckingham Palace, the personal assistant following closely behind.

They came to a door of a different character to the rest. Not waiting, the King opened it and entered. Lindsey stayed outside, getting only a glimpse of the lounge beyond the door, and the adjoining bedroom.

Closing it behind him without a word, Alfred left Lindsey standing alone and without instructions.

He remained for some time, waiting as various functionaries passed on their way here or there, until he went home for the night.

When he returned to work the following day, he found that the King had not left his suite. He proceeded with his work of cancelling the King's appointments, only for that day – a partial compliance with the King's instructions.

For the remainder of that day, Lindsey had no work to do. He spent his time involving himself with the sundry workings of the Palace, becoming familiar with the jobs some of the other staff did.

The next day was much the same, the King remaining in his private rooms, accepting meals, but nothing and no one else.

Lindsey continued to make himself useful in other areas but, with the King offering no instructions of any kind, everyone's workload was smaller.

And the next day was the same.

And the next.

4

English Rose

His Royal Highness Prince Adrian's funeral had been a huge affair, attended by all the great and good in the Royal family, the upper echelons of government, the entertainment industry, the armed forces, and foreign dignitaries.

The King made his first appearance in a week, public or private, to attend his son's funeral, appearing properly groomed, but underfed. His weakened appearance was not lost on the world's media, who reported it the moment they saw him. He avoided all contact with anyone who might have required him to speak, and only opened his mouth to deliver a short eulogy, after which he sat back down, forlorn, and did not speak again.

The larger share of speaking and interacting fell to Princess Frances, who delivered a full and loving tribute, enshrining her brother's memory in a way that resonated with the gathered assembly. After the funeral she arranged an informal press conference in which she apologised for her father's poor showing, and assured the press that after a period of grief he would be back to his full powers. This satisfied some of them, but others would not let the matter rest, pointing out that, while the country was in a state of civil war, its leader could not afford time out for grief or any other reason. The Princess had informed them that matters were in hand, and they need not worry about the direction of the ship of state.

In attendance as well, of course, were the Prince's widow and two sons, and – separately – Olivia Trafford. The young princes recognised her and insisted on introducing her to their mother as their father's stenographer who had had pizza with them. Princess Lillian eyed the strange young woman with suspicion, but greeted her cordially before making an excuse to take her sons elsewhere.

Blair Lindsey stayed close to the King throughout the event, though Alfred made no use of him. When the King left early, leaving Lindsey at the reception, the young personal assistant naturally gravitated to his wife.

Soon, Mr and Mrs Lindsey came into contact with Princess Frances as she was doing her rounds of all the guests.

They bowed to the Princess. "Your Highness, my wife and I are terribly sorry for your loss."

Frances shook both their hands. "Thank you so much Mr Lindsey. I want to tell you how much I appreciate the way you look after my father."

"Well Your Highness, I don't so much look after him as type his letters, take his minutes, and organise his diary. He's a very capable man, and doesn't really need looking after."

"Of course." The Princess looked down at Lindsey's hand, which was clutching his wife's. "And would this be your other half?"

"I beg your pardon, Your Highness. May I introduce my wife, Anita?"

"It's a pleasure to meet you, Mrs Lindsey."

"The pleasure is all mine, Your Highness," Anita said, West Country accent colouring her words. "I'm only sorry the occasion has to be such a sad one. I'd much rather have met you under better circumstances."

"Indeed. So would I. My," she said, looking around, "husband is around here somewhere as well. Perhaps you can meet him some other time. Now, Mrs Lindsey, may I borrow your husband for a little while? I need to look after some of my father's business, which by no coincidence includes Blair."

"Of course Your Highness. Have a good day at work, dear." She gave Blair a kiss and gently pushed him toward the Princess. "He's all yours."

"Thank you Mrs Lindsey."

"Please, call me Anita."

"Anita. I'll try to return him intact."

Lindsey looked back at Anita. They waved at one another as the Princess led him away.

"What 'business' are we looking after, Your Highness?"

"Well, normally my father would send thank-you notes to all the important people who attend an event such as this, wouldn't he?"

"Yes, but all I'd do is draft the thank-you letter, usually from a ready-made template. Recording all the different people at the event, and organising the letters' logistics would be done by some one else. So I don't think you'll need me until you want to draft a letter, which I assume you'll want to do to save His Majesty the stress."

"True, but in the absence of my father I will have to meet all these dignitaries myself. And as you are always at my father's elbow, I'm seconding you to be at mine now. Take notes, keep track of things, look after my diary. My father trusts you, so so shall I."

"As you wish, Your Highness."

For the remainder of the reception Lindsey remained at the Princess's elbow, doing for her what he would normally do for the King. He did not see his wife again until he arrived home, exhausted, late that night.

Prime Minister Hollings waited, standing in his accustomed place in the House of Commons, for the noise to die down.

The Speaker banged his gavel, shouting for order and silence.

"The King will appear," Hollings said, shouting over the receding tumult, "in his own good time. He has been through a lot recently, and we must all do our best to give him the time he needs."

Shouts arose from the benches. "Ridiculous!" "While the civil war tears the country to shreds!" "What does he think we are supposed to do in the meantime?"

"The armed services can see to the civil w– the unrest. Here in government, we continue to conduct business as usual."

"And who is going to sign our bills into law?" An unidentified minister shouted.

"In the absence of the King, we will leave bills unsigned, to be enacted when he is back at work. Now," Hollings said as he waved his hand in front of him to encompass the gathered ministers, "I am ashamed of all of you, getting all up in arms like this. This is not the first time in history that Britain has been ruled by a King, and it is not the first time in history that that King has become incapacitated to the point that Parliament had to operate without him for a time. So get your heads together, and act like men."

A fresh wave of shouted protests arose from the benches, and especially from the female members of Parliament.

Hollings closed his eyes, put his hands to his brow, and shook his head in despair.

Again, the speaker called for order. The commotion subsided.

"If you can't behave yourselves any better than a room full of children for me, I hope you can at least do so for your Princess." The members stared back blankly at the Prime Minister. "Her Highness Princess Frances wishes to speak to address this house."

Yet another wave of cacophonous objections came to the Prime Minister's ears, expressing outrage at the very idea of a Royal in the House of Commons.

Hollings waited for the commotion to die, though this time the speaker found it hard to kill even with her hammer.

"You, my parliamentary colleagues, seem to have still failed to understand the facts of the New Order. His Majesty may go where he wishes. Her Royal Highness is here as his representative, so so may she. It is not a matter for debate."

Taking a sheet of paper from the table in front of him, Hollings held it high. " Rather than deal with all your noise, I shall deal with a few of the more common questions that have been asked of me in private." He put on a pair of reading glasses and held the paper in front of his eyes. "In fact, rather than deal with these questions myself, I will ask her

Royal Highness to answer them. And they are these: 'Has the King abandoned the country?', 'Are we going back to the old order?', 'Is Parliament back in charge?'

"Ladies and gentlemen, Honourable members of Parliament, her Highness the Princess Royal."

Protocol required that they all stood, which they did, but there was little enthusiasm, only a few acknowledging her with a clap as she entered the House of Commons and glided in to the Chamber. The Prime Minister was one of those few offering enthusiastic applause.

Dressed in an elegant pastel suit, she appeared a no less regal figure than her father, standing with patience and poise as the commotion subsided, positioning herself at the centre of the Chamber, exactly between the two banks of opposing benches. Speaking to the members of Parliament filling the green benches and spilling over to stand at either end of the chamber, the Princess's voice was swallowed up by the high ceiling and could not be heard except by those members nearest to her. She reached to her waist and switched on a wireless transmitter connected by a wire to a lapel microphone clipped to her jacket.

"Honourable members of my father's Parliament, I come before you to ask you… no, urge you… no, require you to support my father at this difficult time. I realise that some of you do not particularly favour the monarchy, but I also know that some of you have lost children. Others of you have lost brothers or sisters. Those of you who have not, at least try to imagine the pain my father and I feel, and the effect it has on us.

"But it is especially hard on my father. Many of you remember the toll my mother's death took upon him, and, yes, he hid himself away for several years. But his responsibilities are different now from what they were then, and they press upon him. He knows how much his country needs him, and after an appropriate time of grief he will be return.

"So, to your questions. 'Are we going back to the old ways?' Emphatically not. The New Order is the government of the United Kingdom. It is here to stay. It continues.

"'Has the King abandoned the country?' No! Who could so much as imagine such a thing? My father loves Great Britain as much as he loves life; as much as he loves" – her voice cracked with emotion – "his children.

"'Is Parliament back in charge?' This question arrogates to yourselves authority which has never been yours, an arrogance of which no parliamentarian should ever be guilty. In point of fact, when were you ever in charge? All of you – even you, Prime Minister – were elected by your constituents to represent them. And that you continue to do.

"A true parliamentarian democracy has no person in charge. It is an entity without a head. It is a government that cannot govern, subject as it is to the divided opinions and divided interests of a divided public and a divided membership.

"No, there is no going back. My father has no wish to decapitate the country.

"My father is still your King. And I am still the Princess Royal. My father's parliament would do well to remember this.

"Please direct any further concerns to the Prime Minister. I'm sure he is eminently competent to answer them."

As she turned to leave, made her way through the chamber, and exited, Prime Minister Quincy Hollings led the House of Commons in an enthusiastic appreciation for their Princess, which collectively resembled more of a polite clap.

Hollings stood up and took his place at the table, leaning on it with one elbow. "Now," he said, "continuing today's business…"

"Thank you for coming to see me, General Montgomery," Princess Frances said, standing up from her desk and extending her hand toward the General.

Montgomery executed a curt, formal bow before accepting and shaking her hand. As he released his grip, he noticed Lindsey standing unobtrusively in the corner. "Mr Lindsey, has His Majesty released you from his service?"

Lindsey looked up from his notebook, biting his lip and glancing from the General to the Princess and back again. "Well, His Majesty won't let me into his suite. He won't let anyone in!"

"Blair's working for me," the Princess said, sitting down in her vintage office chair, "until my father has need of him again. It'd be a shame to let his skills go to waste, don't you think General?"

"Er, yes, I suppose so," Montgomery said, still standing. "Now, Your Highness, while it's always a pleasure to see you, I really am incredibly busy, what with running down insurgents and so forth. So what did you wish to see me about?"

"I, er…" She paused, biting her lip. "I wish you to give me a full status report on the Civil War."

"This is… perhaps… slightly irregular, Your Highness. What I mean by that is, I only ever give such reports to your father, and–" The General's expression changed in an instant, and he held a hand up. "You just referred to the uprising as 'the Civil War'. His Majesty never uses that term."

"What is, is. After all, a spade by any other name…" She shrugged. "Now, while my father is, shall we say, incapacitated, you may give his reports to me. I'm sure he'll come back to us soon, but in the meantime the fighting isn't stopping, is it?"

"No it isn't. In fact it's taken some interesting new turns."

"Good. Tell me about them."

Lindsey watched, eyes wide, while the General stood looking intently at the Princess, pausing while her words hung in the air.

"Well, Your Highness," Montgomery said, sitting down with an exaggerated exhalation, "the militia have gone underground. Literally."

Lindsey looked back down to his book, resuming his note taking while the General spoke.

∗∗∗

"Do your loyalties shift," Youngblood said, looking away from the Princess and toward Lindsey, "so easily?"

"My loyalties haven't shifted," Lindsey said from the nearby chair where he sat. "They're first to my Lord and Saviour, then to my wife, and then to my employer."

"Hmm. Technically the correct answer. Now, Your Highness," the Archbishop said, looking back to the Princess who was seated at her desk, and crossing his legs as he leaned back in his chair, "I am a very busy man, as I'm sure you know, so – to cut to the chase – to what do I owe the pleasure of your summons?"

The Princess leaned forward at her desk, clasping her hands together and resting them on the surface. "You and my father are very close, aren't you?"

"Yes." Youngblood cleared his throat. "Yes of course."

"And what do you and he talk about in your frequent consultations?"

"Well, we speak to one another as a man speaks to his friend. He occasionally asks for spiritual counsel, though he is not a particularly spiritual man, and sometimes asks for my take on this event or that event – I do try to keep up with the news – or he talks to me about his family. We had a great deal to discuss concerning your late brother."

"Such as?"

"I may not divulge any confidences, you understand, but His Majesty wondered if he was to blame, as all men in similar situations do. He asked if I thought he had brought his children up properly."

"And?"

Youngblood squirmed a little. "Of what consequence is my answer, Your Highness? Especially as you know the answer to the question better than I."

"Indeed I do. But I'd still like to know how you answered him."

"In truth, I don't remember exactly, though I'm sure Mr Lindsey could exhume it from the minutes. But in general, I told His Majesty the fault was not his, and that he was a good father." Youngblood's eyes narrowed and glinted as he held up his hand to hold off a comment from the Princess. "At moments like those, whatever the truth may be, what do you tell a man who's hurting the way he was? You tell him he was a good father."

"Yes, Uncle Woollie," the Princess said, a snide gloss on her voice, "whatever the truth may be. Because not only do you know as well as I do that he hasn't been a conventional 'good father', but that my brother and I inherited his parenting skills, which is to say none at all. You may only be married to my first cousin once removed, but you have been a part of the family for most of my life, and so you should be able to be more honest with my father."

"Indeed. But," Youngblood said, producing a handkerchief from his pocket and wiping his nose, "sometimes the truth hurts. Not just the hearer, but the speaker." He frowned, putting a hand to his heart.

"Let us change the subject," Frances said in a businesslike tone. "What is the state of the English Church?"

"Ah," the Archbishop said animatedly, "attendance is up. One positive feature of the New Order is the uncertainty it puts into people's hearts, thus prompting them to consider the 'otherness' of spiritual things. And, perhaps surprisingly, our relations with Rome are improving. His Holiness has even said–"

Youngblood's attention was distracted by a slight shaking of Lindsey's head, even as the younger man looked down and wrote in his notebook.

"You have some comment to make, Mr Lindsey?" the Archbishop said.

"Well, it's not really my place to speak here."

"Do carry on Blair," the Princess said.

Lindsey looked at them both, eyes darting back and forth. "All right then. The Church of England was formed specifically to get out from under the yoke of Catholicism, by godly men who sincerely, and with good reason, regarded the Pope as the antichrist. It's ironic that you'd give tuppence for the Pope's opinion. To court his good favour today seems a waste of the blood of men who laid down their lives will-ingly to free Britain from… popery. But I guess I shouldn't complain. At least they bought us four hundred years of Reformation."

The Archbishop smiled condescendingly at Lindsey, turning to the Princess. "Shall we live in the past, or the pres-ent, Your Highness?"

"Yes, thank you Blair. Thank goodness we're not in that position today. Now, do continue Uncle Woollie." She took a deep breath and inclined her head upward to look down at him. "Tell me all about how you advised my father."

"Good afternoon Quincy," the Princess said as she reached across her desk to shake the Prime Minister's hand. "I didn't expect to see you twice in the same week. Please sit down. Now, what can I do for you?" The Princess leaned forward in her chair, resting her clasped hands on the desktop.

"Thank you, Your Highness, for seeing me on such short notice," the Prime Minister said, squirming slightly. "I prom-ise not to take up much of your time. I… trust His Majesty is improving?"

The Princess raised an eyebrow. "No, not much. Is that why you've come to see me, to enquire after the health of my father?"

"No… I mean, yes… I mean…" Hollings straightened his tie and took a breath. "Of course I'm interested in His Majesty's health, Your Highness, but I'm here with my Par-liamentary hat on. To cut to the chase, would His Majesty be well enough – be able to return to work long enough – to sign an act of Parliament?"

"No. Don't think I haven't already tried to persuade him to phase himself back into the land of the living. I've painted word-pictures for him of doom and gloom to illustrate the consequences of continuing as he is, but he's having none of it. His grief will have to run its course."

Hollings slumped in his chair. "That's what I was afraid of. But if he doesn't come back soon…"

"You imagine yourself presiding over the second revolution in as many months. A new world record. There is, however, one way we could put things right. You…" The Princess bit her bottom lip, pausing, perhaps for dramatic effect, or perhaps out of uncertainty. Prime Minister Hollings looked at her, expectant. "You could give the bill to me, and I will sign it into law on father's behalf."

Hollings's eyes narrowed and his brow furrowed. "Do you mean," he said, pausing between each word and enunciating as clearly as he could, "you would be willing to act as Regent while the King is incapacitated?"

"Yes. Regent. That is precisely what I mean. I will rule in my father's name until such a time as he's recovered enough to return." The Princess leaned back in her chair, doing her best to radiate authority and reassurance.

"That could work." The Prime Minister took a handkerchief out of his pocket and mopped his brow. "I'll need to run it past my parliamentary colleagues to see if they'll accept this arrangement."

"That won't be necessary." Princess Frances stood up, gazing down at the Prime Minister. "My father took authority over Parliament. All he needed was the army behind him. I will do the same."

Hollings's eyes widened. "You mean you've–" He took a deep breath. "Am I to understand… that you and the General… That you and the army… That they are on your…" He blotted his forehead with his handkerchief and puffed his cheeks. "Gosh."

The Princess nodded, her cheeks a bit redder than usual. "Give me your bills. I'll enact them – at my discretion, of course."

Sweating, the Prime Minister loosened his tie. "Okay. Thank you, Your Highness."

"Thank you, Randall."

"Quincy." Hollings's face went slightly red.

"But Quincy's your middle name. Why not go by your first name? Randall is much more prime-ministereal."

"I prefer Quincy." The Prime Minister politely wiped his brow again.

"Yes, I know. And I know why," the Princess said with a knowing wink. "A certain shady lady who, in your days as a backbencher, earned you the nickname of 'Randy' from your colleagues. You've done an amazing job living that down. Even becoming Prime Minister. Genius!"

"Alright Your Highness," Hollings said impatiently, "thank you for reminding me. I came clean; I paid my dues; I even reconciled with my wife. Now, I prefer to be called 'Quincy', Your Highness."

"And you can call me Frances, when we're alone together… Randy." She repeated the name again, drawing it out. "Randy. That's a perfectly good name. Americans use it to shorten Randall or Randolph. I think we should use it in Britain. Perhaps it needs an act of Parliament. What do you think, Randy?"

"I'm… not quite with you, Your Highness."

"Frances. Perhaps I can make it clearer to you when you come over to Kensington Palace for your weekly meeting with the sovereign. Just the two of us." Still standing, she held her hand out, indicating the door. "Good afternoon, Prime Minister. Try not to think of me when you go home to your wife this evening."

Hollings stood up, bowed, and left the room, opening and closing the door himself while mopping his brow and running a finger along the inside of his collar.

"Spragg! Bennett!" Corporal Lulworth shouted over to Jimmy and Johnny, who were standing nearby, assault rifles at the ready and waiting for orders. "Come with me, lads."

"Yes sir," the two young soldiers said in unison as they moved toward the manhole down which Lulworth was beginning to climb.

The manhole was located on one of the main roads extending outward from the historic city centre. The floodlit towers of York Minster were visible a few hundred metres away, and floodlights on tripod stands banished the darkness from the area of the manhole to a radius of about five metres. Tens of soldiers were visible in all directions, coming and going, standing by, keeping watch, waiting for orders. The occasional armoured vehicle or Army Land Rover passed by, rattling the ground and the soldiers.

Jimmy and Johnny followed the Corporal down the manhole and were quickly swallowed up by the darkness of the sewer system. Before their eyes had time to adjust to the blackness, the soldiers ahead of them lit flares and dropped them in the ankle-deep sewage, producing brightly flickering red lights from under the murky water, and illuminating floating things that none of the soldiers wanted to see.

Jimmy and Johnny moved forward, keeping the Corporal ahead of them. They passed a couple of engineers who were fixing some wiring to the walls. As the first flares went out, their light was replaced by dimmer but steadier electric lights.

As they continued moving forward, following the Corporal, their boots, socks, and feet became soaked in the run-off from the thousands of sinks, basins, drains, and toilets of the city of York. The foul moisture found its way up the legs of their trousers like wax up a candle's wick, and splashed around with their footsteps, finding its way onto every other part of their bodies.

Before long they came to a four-way junction. They joined three more soldiers who had already tossed flares in the remaining three directions and were now waiting. Some distance behind them, the engineers continued stringing up lights, though they couldn't keep up with Lulworth's team, and some of the flares were dying before the engineers could get there.

"Fredrickson, Paanth, Gorrie, scout these tunnels for a hundred metres, and report back. Spragg, Bennett, deploy your night-vision and keep your eyes on them."

"Yes sir," the five soldiers said in unison as they executed their orders.

Jimmy and Johnny extracted their night vision gear as quickly as they were able given the limited elbow room.

Once his goggles were fitted, Jimmy squeezed past Lulworth. "Sorry sir." He craned his neck into the junction to look right and left, while Johnny surveyed the way ahead.

Resolving in front of him perhaps a hundred metres, the claustrophobic tunnel opened into a larger area, though there was not much of a view of it with Fredrickson filling most of the width and height of the tunnel halfway along. Through a small gap between the sewer wall and Fredrickson's helmet, crouching behind some pumping equipment, a figure hid.

"Tangos directly ahead!" Johnny shouted under his breath, as if trying to control how far his voice would carry. "Tangos ahead!"

"Tangos to the right," Jimmy said as he struggled to look around the corner while sharing the uncomfortable space with the Corporal. "And to the left."

At that, automatic gunfire echoed down the tunnels and chips of brick flew all around the tiny junction.

As Jimmy watched, Paanth collapsed, though the sloping tunnel walls kept him partially upright. Jimmy looked right and saw that Gorrie had also been taken out.

"Man down," Johnny said, still peering ahead.

"Men down," Jimmy said. "Two!"

Lulworth put his hands on Jimmy and Johnny's heads. "Eat that sewage, men!"

"But it's–"

"That's an order, private!"

The two soldiers obeyed, splashing face down into the muck as another volley of bullets and shrapnel sprayed toward them.

Lulworth fell on top of Jimmy, motionless.

The firing stopped.

Prone under his superior officer, Jimmy lifted his head, looking down the field of vision offered by the night vision goggles, and took aim. He squeezed off a few rounds and watched. The not-completely hidden figure fell sideways, and Jimmy fired more shots into him.

"Let's get out of here," Johnny said, "before they get us too!"

"What if our guys are still alive?" Jimmy squirmed out from under the Corporal's body. "At least we know the threat straight ahead is down." He felt Lulworth for signs of life. "Corporal's dead."

"He saved us. Let's not waste it!" Johnny got his feet under him.

"I'm not leaving without Fredrickson, Paanth, and Gorrie."

"How? If we move into that junction, we're dead. At least we know the way back is safe."

They looked back and saw the engineers crumpled near their nearest light fixtures.

"Aw, man!" Johnny kicked at the thick water around his feet, splashing unpleasantness onto the walls. "Those dudes was me mates."

"Sorry. Look, do cops have night vision?"

"I don't know! Do cops have RPGs? Do they have radio jammers?"

The sounds of splashing feet came from the junction's right and left tunnels, pausing only long enough to climb over the fallen Paanth and Gorrie, getting closer fast.

Jimmy and Johnny looked at each other through their awkward goggles, nodded their heads, and made for the junction.

Jimmy facing left and Johnny facing right, they fell sideways into the branching tunnels, firing the instant their night-vision resolved the figures moving toward them. Both men found and downed their marks. They remained where they were, peering down the tunnels for a few more seconds.

"I don't believe you, man," Jimmy said. "You are so mad!"

"Me? Mad?"

"That stunt was totally your idea!"

"No it wasn't, it was yours! I wouldn't have done it but you didn't give me a chance not to." Johnny tried to gesticulate, but there was not space to extend his arms.

"Whatever. Look, you go check Gorrie, I'll get Paanth and Fredrickson."

"Nevermind Fredrickson. I saw him go down. Even in green, it wasn't pretty."

They checked the bodies, and all were dead.

It took them a quarter of an hour to drag the bodies to the wider area where they had originally entered the tunnels, even leaving the dead police – or militia men, or whatever they were – where they fell. Other soldiers helped the two back to street level.

Jimmy sat on the bonnet of an army Land Rover speaking to Colonel Broadley. "They was just sat there waiting there for us. Fredrickson and the others never had a chance." Off to one side some other soldiers were awkwardly lifting the bodies of Fredrickson, Paanth, and Gorrie out of the open manhole. "We got three of them, maybe punched a hole in their defence. Maybe we should've pushed forward, I don't know, but there was only the two of us."

Broadley waited for Jimmy to finish before speaking. "Well I for one am glad you didn't. Better that you came out alive to tell us about it than to push forward and get killed as well. Out of six teams we sent into the sewers, only you two lads have come back."

"Can we go back down Sir? We really wanna get those…"

"Not right now men," Broadley said. "Get back with your unit. Dismissed."

"Yes sir," they said, saluting him. They turned and walked away.

"Some things never change," Jimmy said.

"Yeah, like we're the ones fightin' and dyin', and they don't tell us nothin', innit?"

***

A popular independent betting shop stood on one of the less well-travelled shopping streets in the city of York, sandwiched between a dry cleaner and a fish and chips shop.

Even now, at the wee hours, light filtered in from the Inside this betting shop was a bank of televisions, several worse-for-wear tables, posters advertising various sporting and gambling events, and counters where the punters would line up to place their bets, behind which were tall stools for the bookies to sit on collecting the hordes of money that even a small independent betting shop could produce.

Having been closed for business since the fighting had begun several weeks earlier, the interior had accumulated a layer of dust and neglect to enhance its already somewhat ramshackle appearance.

There were, however, footprints in the dust, tracing a path around the interior of the shop, but centring around two points: the front door, and a hatch, a kind of trapdoor, flush with the floor, just behind the cashier's counter. A clerk might have served customers there for months without ever noticing he stood on the entrance to the basement.

The darkness of night was relieved only by the amber glow of the sodium street lighting outside, as the trapdoor opened, an arm pushing it up from underneath. The arm was followed by and attached to a man. Dressed from head to toe in black lycra, a slim duct-tape-wrapped parcel was attached to his gut and a handgun in a holster clung to his hip. He was followed by several similarly-equipped men and women, emerging onto the shop floor and the layer of dust which covered it.

With no more than the pale illumination of the sodium street-lighting filtering in through the windows, the leader made his orders known through hand signals. Wearing a satin mourning-band as insignia of rank, he moved to the front door while the others stayed at the back. Watching until a patrol of soldiers moved down the street and around a corner, the leader unlocked the door, motioned for the others to follow him, and stepped out onto the narrow street.

The persons in black moved in silence, pressing themselves into shadows as much as possible, until they came to a road where there was a detachment of soldiers centred around an open manhole.

Mourning-Band signalled his group of makeshift commandos, pointing to the various army vehicles parked on the road. The black-clad insurgents slinked unseen to their several targets, sliding on their backs under the vehicles where they tore the packages away from their abdomens with a sound of velcro, attached them to the undercarriages, and slipped away again, still undetected.

They returned to the betting shop, entered, and locked the door behind them. Mourning-Band took a radio from his belt and spoke into it: "Black-five here. The post has been delivered. Standing by."

They descended again into their trap door, leaving such a confused mess of footprints on the floor as not even a Red Indian tracker could unravel.

Jimmy and Johnny walked the streets, as did many other soldiers, patrolling, looking for unusual activity, and making a show of being present. They moved along one of York's less popular shopping streets past a betting shop, a chippy, and a dry cleaner's.

"I wouldn't know where to start," Jimmy said. "I mean where would I find one?"

"They're everywhere man," Johnny said. "Bars, clubs, on holiday in Ibiza, down the pub…" He cocked a thumb over his shoulder. "Even the laundromat."

"No, I wanna find someone I have something in common with."

"Then take some classes. Join some clubs. Join the army!"

"Hah, hah, hah," Jimmy said in a mocking tone.

"There's women in the Army. You have noticed that, right?"

Jimmy pushed Johnny's shoulder, causing him to lose his balance and step off the footpath into the road, at the same moment as a multitude of explosions filled their hearing, some near and some far.

They looked back in the direction they had just come from. Light and shadows cast by flames danced on the sides of the buildings around the nearest junction.

Dashing back to the junction, they rounded the corner and saw four vehicles, one blown to pieces, another overturned, each one an inferno.

Other soldiers were scattered around, one aflame, several more sprawled on the ground unmoving, the rest swaying and disoriented.

Starting with the burning man, Jimmy and Johnny helped in whatever way they could. In moments they were joined and assisted by other soldiers who had been attracted by the noise.

"Report, General," Princess Frances said, looking at the video monitor in Buckingham Palace's situation room. General Montgomery's image was pixelated with compression artefacts, and his voice sounded like an echo in a multitude of tin cans.

He gave his report, concisely describing the situation in York. "For the moment we've pulled back. We're still considering how best to flush them out, but I've only just sent another regiment from Lancashire to help mop things up."

"Countermanded," the Princess said.

"I beg your pardon?" Montgomery blinked several times, raising his brows, eyes wide.

"Bring them back. Events are brewing. They may well be required elsewhere quite soon."

"I see. I was rather relying upon them. We'll need an alternative strategy."

"It's perfectly simple, General. The Yorkists are in an enclosed space. Gas them."

"We have considered that. We ruled out teargas: it's more effective on some people than on others, and in any case one can still fire a gun while half-blind and disorientated."

"I agree," the Princess said. "No point risking our men when there's a much better way."

"We've also looked into some kind of sleeping gas, but–"

"Gas, yes. But no, General, I have in mind something a bit more permanent."

"You–" The General inhaled deeply. "You want us simply to kill them all? Your Highness, they're British, just like you and I."

"When they turned against their country they ceased to be British, as far as I'm concerned."

"Be that as it may," the General said, "that seems to me an overly cruel policy as long as there's a chance we can capture them."

"General Montgomery," the Princess said with a cutting edge, "you were their prisoner. Is it possible you developed some sort of sympathy for your captors?"

Montgomery's jaw dropped. "Certainly not! But I'm uncomfortable administering the death penalty when most of them haven't killed anyone, and none have been tried. If this is the order, I would rather hear it from His Majesty."

"My father is not able to cope with this right now. If we wait until he is all better, which may or may never happen, the underground might gain a lot of ground against us, possibly more cities or even entire counties. Do you want to win, or not?" She held his eyes for a moment through the blocky and cold digital medium. "Very well. Put them to sleep, kill them, collapse the sewers on them, it makes little difference to me. Though I would rather the British taxpayer didn't have to support them spending the rest of their lives in prison. But you're the General. It's your decision. Just sort it out."

"You want me to pick the lock of the King's private apartment?" Reginald, the keeper of the keys, the site manager of Buckingham Palace, had already acknowledged that the door to the King's suite was the only one to which he did not hold a key. "I don't believe you actually have the authority to give such an order."

The Princess took a deep breath, gritting her teeth. "I must check on my father's well-being. What if," she said, leaning closer to Reginald and speaking in a conspiratorial tone, "he were dying in there? What if he were, in fact, dead?"

"But he's not. We send him his meals every mealtime, and we receive back his empty plates. A man who eats all his meals is not dead."

After a few minutes more arguing and invoking, among other things, Reginald's apparent lack of concern for the well-being of his King, he agreed to allow her entry, but only on her solemn oath that she would never implicate him in any way.

It took Reginald a few minutes to get his lock-picking equipment – his mere possession of which came as a surprise to the Princess – and yet a few more minutes to perform the task.

Entering the only rooms in the Palace which were the exclusive domain of the King, Frances closed the door behind her and turned the lock. "Good luck, Your Highness," Reginald whispered to her through the door. She heard his footsteps fading quietly away on the other side.

Inside this door was a small entry vestibule, with another set of doors about two metres in, which stood open. Beyond them was the King's lounge, well appointed with antique furniture, elegant curtains, and tasteful wallpaper.

The King's clothes were strewn all around, and several of the smaller pieces of furniture had been knocked over and remained where they fell.

Worse were the smell and the flies.

In a corner, on the floor, on top of a plastic sheet, was a large mound of food. Slices of roasted meat, Yorkshire puddings, mashed potatoes, sandwiches, chips, gravy, trifles, cakes, all piled high and festering.

The room was lit only by a sliver of daylight entering through a thin gap between the heavy curtains.

Frances moved into the centre of the room, holding her nose and looking around with her mouth gaping open.

She turned to the internal door which led into the King's bedroom, and opened it.

"Father?"

"What are you doing here? How did you get in?" The King's voice was hoarse, weak. He was sitting, perched on the edge of his bed, wearing pyjamas and a dressing gown.

"Would you believe," Frances said, "I crawled in through the ventilation duct?"

Alfred gave a barely audible laugh.

"Father, you need help."

"You think I'm mad, don't you? You think I don't notice the smell, or the flies, or the mess. You think I care nothing for what's going on out in the world. You think I care nothing for you." He looked at her with his penetrating eyes, sunken though they were. "Is that correct?"

"Well," she said, shrugging her shoulders, "basically, yes. What else am I to think? Your reclusiveness and untidiness I can understand, but not this. What other explanation is there?"

He put his hands to his face and rubbed them all around his head. "Explanations, explanations. I am so weary of them. Weary of everything. Weary of life."

"Father, please let me get you some help."

"No. When I can no longer bear this," he said, holding up his hands to indicate his surroundings, "when I can no longer stand the rotting meat or the rubbish, I will ask for help. But for now, there are other things harder for me to bear."

Frances went over to him and knelt beside him. She took his hand in hers and held it to her cheek.

"Your concern is noted, my dear. Now," he pointed at the open door to the lounge, "crawl back through your ventilation duct and leave me."

When the Princess came out of the King's apartments, Blair was waiting for her at the door.

"Oh! What are you doing here, Blair?"

"Sorry to startle you, Your Highness." Lindsey clutched his notebook.

"What do you want?"

"I've only just arrived at work, and I'm reporting for duty at His Majesty's door, as usual. Good morning, by the way. It looks as if you're at work earlier than me." Lindsey pointed at the closed apartment door. "I'm surprised he let you in."

The Princess's eyes followed Lindsey's pointing hand and looked at the door. She looked back at Lindsey, her mouth tightly closed. "So am I." She began walking, and Lindsey followed. "Let's discuss this in my father's office."

Neither one spoke again, except to greet the various functionaries they encountered in the corridors, until they were in the King's office with the door shut.

"My father did not let me in. The only way to gain entry to his apartments was to pick the lock."

"And you were able to do that?" Lindsey raised an eyebrow.

The Princess grinned. "Are you impressed? No, I had some help, I won't say who. You can't pick locks, can you?"

Lindsey shook his head. "Can you not just ask the same person to do it again?"

"No. It may raise suspicions." The Princess sat down.

Lindsey did the same. "What sort of suspicions?"

Frances told Lindsey the salient details of her visit with her father. "I'm worried about him. I want to at least get in there and get his place cleaned up – though I don't know anything about cleaning –"

"I could help there," Lindsey said.

"– but someone else would have to help, and we'd need to take him or her into our confidence." She looked away, shaking her head. "No, I don't want this getting out."

"Why not? He needs help. Why don't we just get him some?"

"It's one thing if the King is indulging himself in a few weeks of solitude after his bereavement. Anyone would understand that; he did it before when we lost my mother, and for longer. It's quite another thing, however, for the King to seem to have gone mad. No one would understand that."

"Do you think he's–" Lindsey choked on his words. His voice cracked as he continued. "Do you think he's mad?"

"No. I think he's merely too proud to ask for help. He knows he'll have to at some point, and he dreads it."

Lindsey released a held breath, and leaned forward in his seat. "Okay. So what can we do for him now?"

"Nothing."

"Nothing? That's not good enough. He needs help. We need to get someone in there."

"Oh yes? Who? Who do we know who's completely trustworthy and discreet? I don't know any such people."

"Well I do," Lindsey said.

"I'm afraid that's not good enough. I can't simply take your word for that."

Lindsey stood up and paced around the room, agitated. "Then why did you even tell me about this?"

"Because I trust you, Blair. My father trusts you, so," she said as she stood up and walked over to him, putting her hand on his arm, "so do I."

"Thank you, Your Highness. I'm happy to have your trust. But what are you trusting me with? If you propose to do nothing about your father – and I understand your reasoning, really I do – then the question still stands: why are you telling me about this?"

"Blair," she said, keeping her hand on his arm and looking into his eyes, "I can't keep everything to myself. I had to tell someone. And you're the–"

"–only person you can trust, I know," he said, backing away from her so her hand fell away from his arm. "I won't betray your trust, unless the King's life is in danger, or I think of a better way to get him the help he needs without weakening his authority. I completely understand that terrible things could happen to the country if he were to be seen in his current state."

"And that's why he trusts you." Frances smiled at him, and then returned to the King's desk. "Now, on to the day's other business."

5

Underground

"Evacuate how? Most of our vehicles have been blown up, sir!" Jimmy smiled as he answered the Captain.

"You've got feet, son. Use them!" Captain Smiley pushed Jimmy so that he stumbled backward.

"Yes sir!" Jimmy set off running in the direction the Captain had indicated.

"Get moving, men!" Smiley gesticulated broadly, urging his troops in Jimmy's direction. He looked back at what he had sent them running from.

The members of the underground – uniformed police, people in ordinary clothing, burly men in ski masks, others in body armour – emerged onto the streets from unknown positions, taking cover behind burnt-out vehicles and anything else that would suffice. They fired automatic weapons and rocket launchers at the surprised troops, and many who carried no weapons threw stones and molotov cocktails.

Captain Smiley waited until all his men had left the area before he followed them, during which time he saw several cut down by gunfire.

As he ran in pursuit of the troops under his command, he felt himself nipped in the leg. His movement impaired, he limped at speed until he was reunited with his men.

They were gathered a point well outside of but within easy sight of the city walls. The men stood watching intently while Captain Smiley struggled onward, and when he was among them he collapsed to the ground.

"Are you okay Captain?" Jimmy knelt beside him.

"It hurts! Oh it hurts! The butterflies," Smiley said through clenched teeth as he waved his arms around him, exhausting himself to the point of panting, "don't let 'em get me!"

"What do you mean Sir?" Jimmy looked down at his own knee which was in contact with the ground. It rested in an expanding pool of blood, running from a wound in the Captain's leg. Jimmy shouted, "Tourniquet!"

Several of the men removed their belts, offering them to Jimmy. He took one and looped it around the Captain's leg, just above the wound. Tightened and fastened, it stopped the bleeding.

The Captain was now unconscious.

Jimmy looked around. "Who's got rank here?"

Looking around at one another, the privates shrugged their shoulders, otherwise making no reply.

"No one? Right," Jimmy said, propping Captain Smiley up into a sitting position against the wall of a planter. He stood up and pointed. "Take cover and set up a defensive front here. Come on guys! We gotta keep our Captain safe – and ourselves!"

The men obeyed Jimmy's orders, forming a human barrier between their fallen Captain and the direction they had just fled from, though no enemies had followed them this far yet.

"Hey Jimmy," one of the soldiers said, pointing at a car across the street, "if we bring that over here we can use it as a barrier to protect the Captain."

"Only if it's got no petrol in it," Jimmy said. "I don't fancy taking cover behind an explosive barrier. Do you?"

"We can drain the tank first. A slow drill would only take a couple minutes to punch a hole in it."

"Okay. And how'll you get it over here?"

A group of men broke a window, turned the steering wheel – which locked as expected – and pushed the front of the car by sheer force of arms and legs sideways so that it was pointing toward the Captain. Then they drained the fuel tank, and pushed it into position to protect him.

Commenting on how easy it had been, they began moving more nearby cars to form a customised defensive barrier they could use in case of attack. Jimmy suggested collecting all the petrol in one place so it could be used as part of their defence if needed.

As they worked, an officer arrived from behind their defensive line, some other soldiers following him. "Captain Hardin," the officer announced. "Who's in command here?"

Several of the men pointed to Jimmy.

"It's not me sir," Jimmy said, saluting Captain Hardin. "It's Captain Smiley, but he's injured. We've radioed for medics."

"It looks, Private Bennett, that the men serving alongside you think you're in charge. What are you boys doing?"

Jimmy explained the barrier they were making.

"Good. Making use of your environment. Your men might as well keep at it. I don't think it'll be needed, but better safe than sorry."

"They're your men now, sir. Er, why don't you think we'll need it?"

"I could give you a field promotion. These men respect you." Hardin pointed toward the city walls. "The enemy have captured the city centre. I think that's all they were after. They've taken a lot of casualties. There can only be a few hundred of them left. Not enough to take the whole city. No, the walls are what they want – what they've always wanted. But don't worry, son. There's no way we'll let 'em keep it. Right?"

"Absolutely right, sir. But no thanks on the promotion. I joined up to be a grunt."

"Okay grunt Bennett, you and your men are now under my command. Here are your orders."

By evening, the army had brought in a full complement of artillery to replace the ordnance that had been destroyed or abandoned within the city walls.

"Yes sir. But…"

Major Weldon faced the younger officer, clasping his hands behind his back. "Something else to say Captain?"

"Well," Hardin said, "not exactly meaning to question your orders sir, but didn't the King forbid destroying any historic landmarks? There must be hundreds of them within the city walls."

"I asked the same question when the Lieutenant gave me these orders. He said he got it from General Montgomery, and that the General had squared it with the Princess Royal. She is running the show now, apparently. Only while the King's out of sorts, of course."

"Yes sir. But I'd hate to be there when His Majesty comes back to work and finds that Her Highness has laid waste to his favourite city."

"Me too," Weldon said. "But let's just follow orders from our legitimate authority, and leave the sorting out to them. Now, get our mortars in place. And while we're at it we'd better do something about all the manholes near us. We don't want the enemy coming at us that way."

"That's easy," Hardin said. "We'll just park our vehicles on top of them. They won't be able to lift the manhole covers. But that won't stop them. Those tunnels run for miles."

"Don't worry, Captain. we've got a plan for that too."

Soon, the soldiers were bombarding the city centre mercilessly and, seemingly, randomly.

Every few minutes each mortar squad was given a set of coordinates for a location they were to avoid hitting, with the threat of severe punishment if they disobeyed. There was some discussion among the men as to what purpose this might serve, but they nevertheless observed the prohibition strictly.

Some return fire targeted them, either from mortar equipment already in the underground's possession – though the army had done their best to remove or disable said equipment during the brief period they controlled the city centre – or weapons left behind when the soldiers had previously withdrawn. In any case, the accuracy of the incoming fire was poor, so there were few casualties.

Meanwhile, other teams were busy examining the manholes. Wherever they found one that concealed a tunnel large enough for men to move through, they planted and detonated demolition charges to collapse them.

The city council building was just inside the city wall, not far from where Captain Hardin was commanding his bombardment. Jimmy and Johnny could not take the direct route, having to find a point along the city wall where they could infiltrate undetected. This took them a considerable distance from their target before they were able to begin snaking their stealthy way through the city streets, avoiding the few militia they were able to see.

All around them mortar shells were exploding, friendly fire which never came close enough to do them any harm due to the GPS equipment feeding their coordinates to the mortar teams.

The intensity of the bombardment soon drove the insurgents away – into the sewers, Jimmy and Johnny presumed – so that the city now seemed completely deserted, even as it was being blown to rubble.

It was not long before they were once again in sight of the council building.

Johnny began walking toward it, in the middle of the tiny debris-strewn street.

"What are you doin', man?" Jimmy sidled along the wall at one side. "Stay in the shadows!"

"Come on. The enemy should more worried about staying undercover than us."

"Yeah, well, better safe than sorry," Jimmy said, following Johnny anyway.

The road was scarcely wider than a man's arm span, and as the two men picked their way along it they stepped over a large amount of wreckage caused by the bombardment. There were masonry blocks, broken glass – and even bits of cars, though there was no evidence of any having been parked on this road.

"See? They ain't out and about. They'd have to have a death wish."

"But they do," Jimmy said as they clambered over a brick wall which had fallen across the road. "Why else would they stand against the entire army?"

Johnny frowned. "I don't know, but they're doing pretty well at it. They're keeping us all on the hop."

As they neared Tanner Row, the larger street running alongside the council building, the ground collapsed under their feet, sinking over a metre before they were able to climb out.

"What just happened?" Johnny shouted.

"I think," Jimmy said, looking down into the trench that now extended across the little road, "a sewer tunnel just collapsed under us."

"Weakened by our mortars, I guess."

"That or we're heavier than we think."

Continuing forward, they emerged onto Tanner Row. The council building was set back from the road, below street-level and isolated by a heavy wrought iron fence, parts of which were blown away and twisted like wire.

The damage to the fence afforded them easy access to the structure, which was itself undamaged.

"It looks kind of like it don't belong," Johnny said, looking around at the extensive damage that had already been suffered by nearby buildings.

"It's got a preservation order – at least until we've finished with it. Let's get in there. We've taken too long already."

Major Weldon and Colonel Broadley sat opposite on another in a modern conference room in a none-too-modern building which they had appropriated and declared their new temporary command centre.

"The underground, militia," Broadley said, "whatever you want to call them, have probably skulked back into the sewers."

"That doesn't make them immune," Weldon said. "Our mortar teams must have collapsed a tunnel or two by now."

"But why are these rebels trying to hold out? They can't possibly believe they can ultimately defeat us."

"I agree. What can a few hundred do against the fully-equipped British army? By sheer force of numbers if nothing else, we'll have to kill or capture them all soon."

"Perhaps they just feel there's no going back. Maybe it's their Masada."

The door opened.

"Major! Look what I've got," a young sergeant said. He held a large piece of rolled-up paper in his hand, which he proceeded to unroll and hold in front of Weldon.

"Fantastic," Weldon said, standing up. He took the paper from the Sergeant and looked around for somewhere to put it. Much of the conference table was already taken up with equipment and maps. Colonel Broadley pushed some of it aside to make room.

As the Major spread the paper across the empty space on the table, it became clear that it was a broad plan of the York sewer system, printed in large format from a digital photograph.

"I presume this means Spragg and Bennett's mission has been a success. As soon as they're out of there you have my permission to extend the bombardment to the council building as well. I never much liked that place anyway." Weldon examined the map. "So Whittle, tell me what I'm looking at here."

Sergeant Whittle traced his finger along various of the sewer routes.

"The main nodes are here, here, here," Whittle said, punching the different locations on the map with his finger, "here, here, here, and here. Those are the points a man could walk through. All the other drainage leading out of the city centre are just pipes."

"Would it be possible for a man to crawl through the pipes?"

"I suppose so Sir," Sergeant Whittle said slowly, stroking his stubbly chin. "But it would be tough – stinky, cramped…"

"Don't you think," Weldon said, "they'd do it if they were fleeing for their lives? Wouldn't you?"

"Yes sir, I would." The Sergeant sighed. "Then add a few more nodes." He marked several crosses on the map with a pencil.

"Good. Organise demolition of these nodes. Collapse them all. Then we'll cut off all routes of escape." Major Weldon stopped, looking into the distance. "We'd better send in someone with a white flag. Offer them one last chance to surrender. Otherwise they're all going to die, and I'm not comfortable with that. They're still British, after all. See to it. There should be ample time to get a negotiator in and out."

While the explosives were being placed, a team of unarmed soldiers ventured inside the city walls and spread out, carrying makeshift white flags and searching for any representative of the insurgents. Several of the soldiers walked the streets, making their presence as obvious as possible, while the rest ventured into the tunnels.

It was not long before one of the emissaries in the tunnels, a young corporal named Granger, made contact with the leader of the underground, one Mr Samuel Phelps.

Granger explained to Phelps that there would be no escape, and that unless they surrendered he could not see any way they could survive.

The underground leader listened with patience, and then excused himself, saying he would have to confer with his superiors.

Making his way through the narrow tunnels as a fine rain of silt and grit and fragments fell occasionally from the ceiling, Phelps squeezed past many armed and sweaty people before emerging into a larger space – a room – equipped with ammunition stores, cots, shelves of canned food, and a messy workstation. Several men were in here as well.

"Out!" Phelps said, closing the door and cutting himself off from the tunnel. He sat down, opened up a laptop computer, clicked the mouse, and typed in a password.

After a thirty-second delay, a sound came from the computer's speakers. "Hello Samuel. It's good to hear from you."

The voice had the distinctive hollow sound of audio compression and encryption.

"And you, Sir Patrick," Phelps said, leaning toward the computer screen.

"So, what can I do for you?"

Phelps briefly explained the situation, and the army's offer of surrender. "I think we should accept Sir."

"If that is a joke, Samuel, it's not funny."

"It's not a joke Sir. I only thought –"

"Samuel," Sir Patrick snapped, "I thought you believed in our cause."

"I do! And I would gladly lay down my life to remove the monarchy from Britain once and for all. But this is just a useless last stand, and we'll all probably be dead soon if we don't surrender."

"I take your point," Sir Patrick said more calmly, "but what you are not aware of is that help is on the way."

"Help?" Phelps flashed a tentative smile, excitement creeping into his voice. "What? Who?"

"I can't give you any details. I know this is a secure line, but still, you never know – but relief is coming soon. Trust me, Samuel. You just need to hold out a little longer."

"We will! Thank you sir. Samuel out." He closed the laptop, stood up, and left the room.

Making his way back through the tunnels, soon he was with Corporal Granger again. "No deal. Sorry."

The soldier stood agape for a moment. "You're having a laugh, right? You can't possibly be serious. Do you all want to be killed?"

A fine shower of debris fell from the ceiling.

"It's not us who're going to be killed," Phelps said, looking up at the unstable ceiling while at the same time exuding belligerent confidence. "Go tell your General, or whoever, that it's you who'd better surrender."

Granger took a breath and opened his mouth as if to

speak, looked down at Phelps's weapon, and closed his mouth. He turned around and walked away from Phelps, looking over his shoulder often until the other man was out of sight.

Corporal Granger stood before Colonel Broadley, making his report on his encounter with Samuel Phelps.

The Colonel sat in a chair at the conference table – where the penciled crosses on his sewer system map had all been replaced with thick red ones – looking up at the Corporal. Major Weldon sat near him.

"Extraordinary," Broadley said, leaning back in his chair and sighing. "What could he have meant by that? Major Weldon, are there any signs of militia reinforcements on the way from any direction?"

"Nothing sir. Not a sausage."

"Granger, is there any chance Phelps might have been…" Broadley twirled a finger around his ear and whistled a two-tone trill.

"Loopy, sir?" Granger shook his head. "I'm no psychologist, but he seemed to have most of his marbles."

"Hmm. Thank you Granger. That'll be all."

Granger saluted and left.

"Well," Broadley said, "that doesn't make it any easier."

"No sir." Weldon's nose twitched. "Still, our duty is to quash the enemy, isn't it?"

"Of course it is, Leo. And we will. It's just a classic problem, and I hate it: we have to kill an enemy who wouldn't even be fighting us if they weren't under the sway of some other person who's playing with their lives. Phelps is calling the shots for the Yorkists, but some one else is calling the shots for Phelps."

"Who?"

"That's the big question." He sighed and rubbed his eyes. "Right. Resume bombardment. Finish them off."

***

Across the city, buildings were blown apart, firestorms generated, craters created, and targets selected without regard for their world-heritage-site status.

The routes of the sewer tunnels were carefully targeted, and visual evidence gained that they were collapsing, leaving trenches and sinkholes, turning the once-beautiful city into a no-man's-land. Not even the Minster was exempt – though its towers still stood, enough damage was inflicted on its structure as to make its future uncertain.

When the city centre was deemed to have been rendered completely unsuitable for human habitation, the Colonel ordered the destruction halted.

Scouts were sent in to ascertain if there were any remaining signs of life, and to apprehend any survivors. There were few to be found, though it was suspected that many more would be trapped under the rubble of the tunnels.

"York is ours," Colonel Broadley said in his communication to General Montgomery, "for what it's worth."

"I understand," the General replied over the video link-up in Broadley's conference room. "Don't worry. The responsibility is mine, and Her Highness's."

Princess Frances sat at her father's desk. Spread out in front of her was a large assortment of bills sent to her from the House of Commons.

For several hours now, she had been reading the bills in a cursory fashion in an attempt to discern which ones for were for the benefit of the country, which for the benefit of vested interests, which for the benefit of ministers of Parliament, and which were intended to limit the sovereign in some way.

Thus far she had found several of every variety, and others besides. Some were well thought out, others ill-conceived, and some simply stupid, to her politically untrained eye at least.

Nearby, Lindsey busied himself, while waiting for any meaningful instructions from the Princess, poring over his notebook in which he assembled and edited the minutes of the various meetings to which he had been party.

The Princess dropped the tip of her pen into its ink well with a small splash of ink and a frustrated noise. She removed her reading glasses and looked at Lindsey. "Why don't you use a computer for that? Anyone else would. We have a significant IT budget in the Palace, you know. You'd might as well use it."

Lindsey lowered his notebook and pencil. "Sorry, Your Highness. I suppose I'm just old-fashioned. I prefer pencil and paper. When I'm finished with this I'll let the typist have it, so don't worry. The IT budget won't go to waste."

The telephone on the King's desk rang.

Lindsey stood up without delay and answered it.

"Yes? Oh… Very well. Connect him please." Lindsey waited a moment before speaking again. "Good afternoon, Mr Vice President. Or is it morning there? I'm Blair Lindsey, His Majesty's personal assistant. Her Highness the Princess Royal is here. I'll ask her." Looking at the Princess, "It's Mr Tyler Seago, the American Vice President, Your Highness. Would you like to speak to him?"

"Yes, thank you Blair." Princess Frances took the phone from him with a polite smile. "Tyler, how are you and Carol? It's been too long."

Lindsey held his finger over the speakerphone button, making eye contact with the Princess. She nodded, and Lindsey pressed the button.

"– to let you know, just out of courtesy." The vice president's voice sounded like one that would have been more at home hawking hot dogs at a Coney Island snack stand, in line with his working-class New York heritage, rather than politely addressing world leaders on the telephone. "We – that's my boss and I – trust you'll make time in your busy schedule to see Mr Stapleton."

"Of course, normally it's always a pleasure to see the ambassador." The Princess frowned. "But at this moment I've got rather a lot on my plate. I should be able to fit him in in about a week…"

"My boss and I don't care how big your lunch is." A cold edge came into the vice president's voice. "The ambassador needs to be seen. Like I said, treat him as if he's the president. He speaks for him, and you wouldn't keep the president waiting for a week would you?"

"No, I don't suppose I would," she said. "But the fact remains that the ambassador is not the president."

"I said, Frances, to treat him as if he is. This… request… comes directly from the president."

"Then perhaps he should be speaking to me himself."

Vice President Seago laughed under his breath. "The President's a very busy man. In fact, so am I. And I'm beginning to feel I'm having my time wasted. I gotta go now. I'll catch up with you later, Frances. Good morning. I mean, good afternoon."

"Good-bye, Tyler," she replied with a sigh. "Remember me to Carol."

Lindsey stopped writing long enough to press the button to end the call for the Princess.

She took a deep breath and let out a deep sigh. "His wife is the only good thing about that man. Well, Blair, you had better make us an appointment with the American ambassador."

The United States ambassador to the United Kingdom, Mr Edward Stapleton, sat at the coffee table in the King's office. Opposite him, on the sofa, sat Princess Frances. A china tea service was laid upon the table. Ambassador Stapleton's cup rested on the table in front of him, while the Princess held her saucer in one hand and a cup near her lips in the other. Lindsey sat in his accustomed corner, writing in his notebook.

Stapleton was tall when standing upright, lean, and well-dressed in a dark suit. His face bore the chiselled features of a film star, and his straight dark hair, though well-kept, repeatedly fell in a comma over his forehead, which he repeatedly pushed back with his left hand.

"Perhaps the hardest problem for us to overcome, Your Highness, is that your government has not actually been recognised formally. Neither by the United Nations, nor the United States, nor most other G20 nations. In fact, Your Highness – though I hesitate to say it – your father's regime could be considered, in some circles, to be illegal."

The Princess took a sip of her tea. "Edward, the United Kingdom is a sovereign nation, and the legality of its government is to be determined here, at home."

"With all due respect, Your Highness, from America's point of view Great Britain used to be a sovereign nation, but she has recently suffered a coup d'état. She is, you might say, up for grabs."

"Nonsense! She's a nation under her King, as she has always been. The manner of government has changed, but all the same people are still in place, still doing their jobs. Elected representatives continue to represent their people. Town, city, and county governments continue to bid for budgets as they've always done."

"Surely you don't mean to tell me – with respect, Your Highness – that nothing has changed? That would disagree with all the evidence of my ears and eyes, and yours too."

"Of course some things have changed, Edward. This kingdom now adheres more closely to the principles enshrined in her national anthem. 'Send him victorious, happy and glorious, long to reign over us'. That's exactly what is happening."

"Your Highness, I am, of course, discussing this with you out of courtesy. Your father is, according to you, the lawful ruler here. It's with him I'll need to speak. Between just you and I, we can't settle anything."

"I cannot believe that you don't know my father is unwell. He simply can't speak to you right now."

"He must. Give us access to the King, or there's no way we can negotiate."

"Negotiate?" Princess Frances put her cup in her saucer, and the saucer on the table. "Negotiate what, precisely?"

"I'm sorry Your Highness, but that is a matter between the US State Department and His Majesty. I'm afraid I can say no more."

"Edward! You've never spoken to me like this before."

"Again, I'm sorry. But this isn't a party at the embassy. Were not hobnobbing over champagne right now. There are stakes here. I'm an ambassador, and you're a statesman. It's a different relationship than our usual."

"Then can you not give me a bit more detail – as a friend? I'll need some idea what the stakes are. It might give me a little more leverage with my father."

"Very well, Your Highness. Anything I say now is strictly off the record. If it's quoted, I'll deny I ever said it."

Frances looked over at Lindsey. He finished off a sentence, closed his book, and put his pen away. She looked back at Stapleton. "Proceed, Edward."

"Well, this administration is very concerned with the state of things in Great Britain. The Civil War is a particular concern. As you're no doubt aware, the United States has a very great deal of financial interest in the UK, much of which is threatened by destabilisation."

"That situation will be under control very soon."

The ambassador shrugged, which made a lock of his hair fall over his forehead. He pushed it back. "That's as may be – as your friend, I'm perfectly happy to believe you – but that's not good enough for the president, who has American business concerns with significant investments in the UK clawing at his back right now.

"And the Civil War – may I call it a 'peasant uprising' for the moment? – in what's normally the world's most stable country could have a devastating influence in other nations where the peasants are contemplating rising up. I hope not, but it could lead to a chain reaction, affecting US interests in many parts of the world.

"And even if that fear comes to nothing, the matter of a restored monarchy is making waves in every country where there are impotent monarchs – Kings like your father who have for longer than anyone can remember wielded no power over their subjects. How many more will follow your father's example, again threatening US interests across the globe? There are even states which have never had a king suddenly eyeing up potential candidates.

"So you see, there is definitely a lot at stake." He again pushed back the comma of dark hair from his brow.

"I see," the Princess said, frowning. "Thank you for your candour. I admit I've heard some of these rumblings myself. I personally consider these possibilities somewhat remote. And I absolutely can not believe that my father wouldn't have considered these things when he was planning his... take over. He is a very thorough man."

"Which is exactly why," the ambassador said, "I must speak with him. He's the only one who knows the full picture. Or at least, the full picture as he sees it. I can't imagine it'll actually change the President's point of view, but he's willing to listen."

"Then I will certainly make every effort to bring him to the table." The Princess again picked up her cup and saucer, a barely perceptible tremor causing the china to rattle for an instant before she put the cup to her lips and drew a tepid sip. "But I've already tried to reach him, and failed."

"You must reach him!" The ambassador's brow furrowed and the corners of his mouth tightened. "You absolutely must."

"Why? I can probably guess the sorts of things you cowboys might do against us, but I'd appreciate it if you'd spell it out clearly."

He pushed his fingers back through his hair even though none had fallen into his eyes. "I haven't been party to those discussions – if there've been any such discussions. Just go with your best guess. It won't be far from the truth."

The discussion ended, the Princess and the ambassador took their leave of one another, and he departed.

"Well Blair, I suppose we'd better try to get through to my father. While I'm persuading Reginald to pick the lock for me again, you get together whatever you think you might need to clean up his suite."

Later they met at the King's private apartment door. Reginald picked the lock while Princess Frances and Lindsey looked on. When he had finished he was dismissed.

They entered the suite, and the Princess went into the bedroom to find the King.

Immediately setting to work on clearing away the mess, Lindsey pulled a rubbish bin behind him.

After only a few minutes he had deposited the pile of uneaten food in the bin and begun tidying up. All the while, the sounds from behind the closed door of the King's room began as muted conversation, and grew into raised voices, with the King doing most of the shouting.

"Get out!" King Alfred's voice rang loud and clear through the closed door.

The Princess's answers were muted and unintelligible to Lindsey.

"Get out!"

Frances burst out of the King's bedroom, her face locked into a snarl. "That man!" she shouted as she slammed the communicating door and stormed out of the apartment, her stride down the corridor audible for some distance.

Lindsey continued his tidying, there being a long way to go before having the place in shape.

The bedroom door opened again. Lindsey looked at the King, framed in the doorway. His features were drawn, and his beard had grown. Haggard in his well-worn pyjamas, his bony frame held the garments up like a coat hanger.

"You go too, Blair," the King said, his voice strained and gravelly.

"But, Your Majesty," Lindsey said, showing the King the articles of clothing he was holding, "can't I stay and help you? I promise not to get in your way. Please? I'm worried about you."

"No," Alfred said, casting his eyes down to the floor. "I don't need you. Now go."

Lowering the things he was holding, Lindsey's face collapsed. He put the items in a pile he had started in the corner. "Well, please call me if there's anything I can do for you, Your Majesty."

Shaking his head, the King quietly said, "Go. Now."

Backing away and out the door, Blair pulled it closed, pausing just short of allowing the bolt to click home.

Lindsey pushed the door open again. "Your Majesty–"

"Go!" The King's voice thundered, and Blair reflexively pulled the door shut, the latch clicking home with finality.

"That didn't go well, did it?" The Princess began walking around the perimeter of the King's office.

"No ma'am," Lindsey said, standing near the door with his hands clasped in front of him, "it did not."

Frances continued to pace the floor, her eyes aglaze as if they were about to well up. "I can't stand to see Father like that." She put her hand over her mouth and cast her eyes down, her brow tightening.

"Neither can I," Lindsey said, frowning. He put one hand in his pocket, fingering his keys and coins, and ran the other hand through his short ginger hair. "What can we do for him though? He won't accept any help from us or anyone else, and the ambassador proved that we can't show him to anyone until he's better." He growled in frustration.

Still walking aimlessly around the room, hiding her eyes by looking at the floor, not speaking, she stopped in front of Lindsey. She inhaled and exhaled a great sigh, shaking her head.

After a silent pause and without warning, she threw herself upon Lindsey, putting her arms around his neck and pressing her forehead onto his shoulder.

With tentative hesitation he wrapped his arms around her, patting her back with his hand in a sympathetic motion while a glaze of uncertainty came and went across his eyes.

The Princess clung to her functionary, her breathing slowed and she closed her eyes, resting in his embrace.

Lifting her head from his shoulder, she looked into his sympathetic blue eyes with her sad and tired eyes.

Moving quickly, she raised her head and pressed her lips against his, gripping him tightly.

As the Princess kissed Lindsey, he squirmed, and in a moment had snaked his way out of her grasp.

Lindsey reached for the door handle, but as he turned it she moved quickly, squeezing herself into the space between him and the door, pressing her body against his.

He took a step backward, shaking and holding his breath. "Your Highness, please – don't do this wickedness."

"Wickedness, is it?" She leaned back against the door, holding her hands behind her back, her face a picture of dejection as she gazed up at him. "How can you say that when I'm baring my need to you? I live a lonely life – even though there are people around me all the time. But then you came into it. You gained my trust, and I hope I gained yours. That trust leads somewhere, Blair. It leads here," she said, gesturing with her hands to indicate herself, her soul, her body. "I want you, Blair. I need you. Stay with me."

"You did have my respect, Your Highness, but…" He stopped, backing away from her, his face reddening to complement his ginger hair, his breath quickening. "Yes, what you're asking is wickedness."

She scowled, clenching her eyebrows and her teeth. "How dare you say such a thing to me."

"All right, sin then." His eyes darted and he pushed a hand through his hair. "No matter what you want to call it, I can't do what you want."

"Oh no?" she snapped. "Why not?"

"Because…" He held his hands in front of him, moving them around in a nervous motion, grasping at the air. "Because I'm not married to you. And to add to that, I am in fact married to someone else. And so are you!"

Her expression softened a little. "Blair, as I'm sure you know, there is a long and proud tradition of royalty… fraternising, shall we say, with the staff. And often the staff do very well out of it. Don't miss your opportunity – I can take very good care of you, and of your family."

"No. I'm sorry to have to refuse you, Your Highness, but there's really nothing else I can do."

"Oh, but there is," the Princess said with a snarl. "You can submit. My father might never come out of this funk he's sunk into, which would effectively leave me as Queen." The Princess stepped close to Lindsey, taking hold of the lapels of his jacket. "Would you rather risk my wrath?"

Twisting himself out of her grip, he slipped past her, making another attempt at the door.

She reached out, grabbing again for his jacket, and laid hold of the collar with a firm grip.

Lindsey raised his arms and twisted downward, the satiny lining of the coat enabling him to slip out of it completely, leaving her holding the dark jacket in her clenched fist.

Springing up from his crouch, Lindsey twisted the door handle, pulled it open, and bolted from the King's office.

Frances stood in the doorway, quaking with anger. She threw the garment on the floor and slammed the door so that the entire wing felt it.

The next morning, Lindsey never reported for work – at least, not to the Princess.

Accompanied only by a bodyguard, she called on General Montgomery for a special meeting.

"Where's young master Lindsey? I thought he was working for you during the King's absence."

"He was. I dismissed him. He didn't provide adequate service."

"Oh," Montgomery said, raising his eyebrows. "I understand His Majesty always found him to be most efficient."

"Well, to each his own. I believe he's still in the Palace somewhere, if you'd like his services. Now, to business."

She described in detail her meeting with Ambassador Stapleton. Montgomery interrupted occasionally to ask clarifying questions.

"Most interesting," was his only comment when she had finished. He asked after the King.

She told of having met him and of his unconsolable grief and belligerence. Averring that it was difficult to gain access to him, she carefully omitted references to lock-picking, his refusal to eat, his wretched state of hygiene, or being driven from his presence.

The General thanked her for her time, and requested to be kept informed of any further developments.

Princess Frances consulted her diary which Lindsey had left in the King's office and navigated her day without missing any appointments.

At one point she spotted Lindsey and looked icily at him while he talked with an MI8 operative in the Situation Room.

"But they're all dead," the Princess pled. "And everywhere else they're surrendering."

Sitting in a corner of the King's office, Olivia Trafford sat, taking notes in a stenographers' notebook.

Ambassador Stapleton shifted in his chair, waving away the comment with his hand. "A few have surrendered. It's certainly not universal, as you well know. And you had to raze York to the ground to achieve even that."

The Princess rose from her seated position behind her father's desk. While attempting to affect a humbly pleading posture, her inbred pride could not be fully hidden. She held her hands out, palms up. "Surely you can see, it's only a matter of time now. We are on the verge of finishing this."

Stapleton straightened his tie. A comma of hair fell over his forehead. "While I find that difficult to believe, the President finds it impossible. Sanctions are coming. The only way it can be avoided is to give us the King."

Frances blinked. Her hands dropped to her sides. "I beg your pardon? What do you mean to do with him?"

Stapleton held a restraining hand up. "Of course I mean, give us access to the King." He pushed the out-of-place hair back.

"I see," the Princess said, sitting down again. "There may be another way. I could take you as my hostage. You're in my palace, and at my mercy."

The ambassador smiled. "I can think of little that would delight me more than to be your prisoner, Your Highness. However, I think it would concern the president very little, and probably produce the opposite to the effect you intended. Indeed, you could make hostages of all the American expats currently living on your soil, but it'd do no good. Perhaps the previous administration would have been cowed by such things, but not the current one. You remember our recent little incursion into Mangaratu, don't you?"

Miss Trafford looked up at the Ambassador, stopping writing, then resumed.

"As yet I've had no success persuading my father. But I will. I only require more time."

"I'll convey your words to the president, and do my best to persuade him." Some hair again fell over the ambassador's forehead, refusing to stay where he left it.

"Then I won't keep you from your embassy any longer." Frances stood up, extending her right hand to the ambassador across the desk. "Until this matter is behind us."

The ambassador stood, pushing the unruly lock of hair back with his left hand and shaking her hand with his right. "Let us hope so." He released her hand and bowed. "Your Highness."

The Princess watched as Stapleton reached the door in two strides. She glanced at Miss Trafford, who caught the Princess's eye, took the hint, and hastily got up, opening the door for the ambassador.

"She's a stenographer," the Princess said to the departing Ambassador, "not a manservant."

Miss Trafford closed the door.

"You really must be quicker off the mark," Frances said with a frown.

Sitting down again, the Princess stared at a picture on the far wall, stroking her chin.

"Excuse me Your Highness, but your next appointment is due."

The Princess looked at her with expressionless indifference. "One does not speak to a princess unless one is spoken to. Is that understood?" Frances cleared her throat. "I am aware of my appointments, and I will keep them waiting for as long as I wish."

"It makes a change from tunnels," Sir Patrick said.

He, a Police Commander, and Chester walked past ranks of AS-ONE members standing to attention as if for their commander-in-chief.

The wide-open interior space of the unused aircraft hanger was filled with ranks of uniformed police militia, except for a dais equipped with a podium and loudspeaker system. Making a somewhat cramped parade ground for the large paramilitary force, it for the moment allowed the troops a respite from training and indoctrination exercises while Sir Patrick did his inspection.

"Well done, Commander." Sir Patrick clapped the officer on the shoulder. "A fine force of men you're keeping here."

"Yes sir," the Commander said, "well-trained and ready for anything the King and his rabble throw at us. Only–"

Sir Patrick stopped walking, clasped his hands behind his back, and stood facing the Commander. "Only?"

"Well sir… I– I mean, the men…"

"Out with it, son."

"The King, the Princess, General Montgomery – whoever – laid waste the entire city of York. It makes some of the men a little – I don't know – apprehensive. The army have more firepower than we do." He continued under his breath. "And should we really be sending our men to their deaths?"

"I understand." Sir Patrick let his hand fall from the policeman's shoulder. "You think we were defeated at York. The men have doubts. Don't worry. I'm going to address those issues in my speech."

"I wish you would, sir."

"No better time than the present."

Sir Patrick stepped confidently, magisterially, onto the dais and took his place behind the speaker's lectern.

Thunderous applause surged up from his assembled followers.

Fully extending his arms upward, fists in the air, Sir Patrick soaked up the exaltation.

He lowered his hands a little, palms downward. The crowd quietened.

"We are here to end the monarchy!" Not all, but many in the crowd applauded. Again he held out his hands to silence them. "Some of you might be saying, 'the King's not so bad'. Well, I feel differently, but if he's all right, what about his heirs? How long will it be before we have a cruel and wicked tyrant ruling over us with his iron fist? We've already killed many of the King's men, at least as many of theirs as they've killed of ours. Where will it stop? Only with the King and his heirs at our mercy or dead at our feet."

A few among the crowd allowed their worry and uncertainty to show, but most stood stony faced, and a large number smiled.

"It's not for nothing that your local pub's probably called 'The King's Head'. In past times, the anti-Royalists – our lot! – marked out their territory by naming their local hostelries. The meanings of those names has been lost in time, but they're significant. If they wanted the King's head, they said so in the name of their pub. But that's enough history – except for this: Kings and Queens are tools of oppression. The only monarchy where the existence of a royal family can't come back to bite them is Russia, and that only because they killed every last one of them. As long as their blood is running in their veins instead of in rivulets on the ground, we cannot rest." Sir Patrick surveyed the crowd. Some cheered, some smiled, some were stone-faced, many were incredulous. "Is this mere bloodlust? No! This is for the preservation of freedom! This is so every man woman and child in Great Britain can lay down to sleep in peace and safety. Do you think Britain was really safe for those few centuries the monarchy were under submission to Parliament? Apparently not! They've been plotting to get their country back, scheming behind the scenes with almost limitless patience, until they could rise again to dominate their people. Will the King and his heirs be satisfied with merely governing us? I don't think so. Absolute power corrupts absolutely. How long will it be before those who cross the King begin to hear that cry which has gone unheard for so many years: 'Off with his head!'? Mark my words, it won't be long before every word we say will have to be spoken with utmost caution. For how many can speak against a tyrant and expect to keep his freedom – or his head? None!

"Yes, we will have to get our hands dirty. We will have to kill. And, for many of us, our consciences will scream against it. But we must steel ourselves. Our children's children depend on it.

"Royalty is like a dangerous weed. Unless it is pulled up by the roots and destroyed, it remains latent in the soil, and will spring up again.

"Now, we've come this far. There can be no going back. We are now fully committed to going forward. Don't believe any of the rumours you've heard about amnesties, or fair trials. In their eyes, we're traitors, and they will shoot us without a trial if we let them. We will not let them. This is not our choice. The fates have chosen for us."

Sir Patrick paused, making eye contact with many in his audience, seeing some squirm while others remained stolid.

"But that's no terrible thing. If we were not fully fitted, fully committed to the task before us, then how long before the King would lay waste the entire country? He's already destroyed York. Yes, the city lies in ruins, like the cities of Germany were laid waste by our bombs in the last world war. Heaps of rubble. The cathedral's a no-go area now, in danger of collapsing at any minute. And under that rubble lie our brothers! He destroyed the entire city just to get us. Are we going to look on in docility while he razes all our great cities to the ground? I say no!" He punched the air with his fist, raising his voice. "Did our brothers give their lives for nothing? I say no! Will we be cowed in fear? I say no!

"We are outgunned, yes, but weapons don't tell the whole story! We can out-think them. We are creative, where the military mind is not! We have many assets, many resources: hackers, demolitions experts, climbers, divers, gunsmiths, and more. Our skill set is matched only by our commitment.

"And doesn't His Majesty's willingness to lose an entire city tell us that he's desperate? That we've got the army on the run?

"We will hit them where they live – and where we hit them, they will die!"

Sir Patrick raised his fists high.

Acclamation filled the charged atmosphere. Many in the crowd raised their fists over their heads, emulating their leader, and few appeared afraid now.

He motioned for silence. "Thank you my friends – my brothers. May whatever gods you pray to bless our struggle and ourselves."

Stepping down from the dais, Sir Patrick rejoined Chester and walked back to his vehicle, waving at the crowd the whole time.

The car was no-frills, mid-size, nondescript, economical. Sir Patrick and Chester sat in the back seat. Two burly bodyguards occupied the driving and passenger seats.

"I'd say that went very well," Sir Patrick said as the car began moving and left the hangar. Outside, the flight line of the abandoned airstrip, rife with weeds, offered no clue – save for the moving car – that it was in use, much less that a large detachment of underground militia were gathered there.

"I concur, Sir Patrick," Chester said, sitting calm and collected next to his boss. "And yet, I can't help but feel sorry for those men. I mean, do you think they bought it?" Though his speech was calm and even, Chester's cheeks and ears burned red and his brow was damp.

"Why Chester, is that doubt? Sympathy, I hear coming from your lips? The time for any squeamishness is long past, my Lieutenant."

"No. No sympathy, doubt, or squeamishness, sir. Only pragmatism. You just inspired those men to believe in something. Something that may never happen. Do you think they can actually win a war against the combined might of all the British armed forces?"

"You're thinking of their greater firepower. Well, greater firepower has often been sent packing with its tail between its legs. It's happened to Britain, to France, America, Russia, and lots of other countries. A smaller, less equipped force can win over a larger better equipped one. It's only a question of having greater conviction and commitment than the enemy."

"Yes sir, but does York not prove that they do have the commitment? I mean, they levelled the city. British troops killed British subjects on British soil, and destroyed an entire British city in the process. If that's not commitment… Well, don't you think it is?"

"I take your point Chester, but what terms do you think the army would give us? Treason is traditionally punishable by death – though the law has gone soft nowadays, I don't think I'd get off with less than life in solitary."

"That may be, sir, but I wonder if our members – I mean soldiers – would get off easier. Perhaps it's worth considering for their sakes." Chester's hand was quaking. He hid it from his superior's view.

"All I am doing is for their sakes. For their sakes, and for the sakes of all the British people – even if they don't understand – we must bring down the King. I will fight for this cause, to the very last drop of my blood."

"By which, sir, you mean 'their blood'. Because it's they who are on the front lines."

"Yes. I do mean that. The men and I are one. We share a common goal, a common purpose. Their blood equals my blood." Sir Patrick looked sideways at Chester. "But you, my friend… take note, if one is not with me, one is against me."

"Really sir, you can't possibly question my loyalty. We've worked together too long for that. I mean, if we can't be candid with one another... I'm just making sure I understand the plan. After all, I can't back you up if I don't know what you're thinking." Chester looked at the driver and his counterpart. "Are you men clear? How do you feel about all this?"

"I trust Mr Blackwell," the driver said. His counterpart remained still, watching the road.

"This young man is so 'on side'," Sir Patrick said, "that he won't even call me 'Sir Patrick', only 'Mr Blackwell'. I know the King will have withdrawn my knighthood by now – but I use it, I suppose, to make a point."

Chester smiled and nodded. He kept his quaking hand out of Sir Patrick's view.

6

Division

For the next two weeks, the underground rose up in Edinburgh, Glasgow, Belfast, Londonderry, Manchester, Liverpool, Birmingham, Leeds – all of the United Kingdom's major cities with the exception of London.

The Armed Forces were stretched to their limit. All British troops abroad had been brought home to fight on home soil, and now the whole of the British military forces were engaged in a war against their own countrymen – a situation with which few found easy.

The soldiers were accustomed to guerrilla warfare in places where urban and societal infrastructures had already collapsed – Kosovo, Iraq, Afghanistan, and the like – but fighting in modern, fully equipped, fully populated cities was not a normal part of their remit.

To which was added the fact that they were fighting against their own countrymen – a disturbing thing for soldiers trained to fight in foreign places.

To which was added the further fact that destruction of property was to be kept at a minimum. Princess Frances and General Montgomery had both expressed profound regrets at the destruction of York, and neither were in a hurry to make such a decision again.

These caveats had the effect of rendering the military response to the paramilitary offensive ineffective to fight back or destroy the enemy.

For the most part, the affected cities had become divided into militarised zones and, as the partisan forces had come to call them, "liberated zones".

It made little difference to the local residents which zone they found themselves living in. Very few of these were willing to take a side, many of them having commented on the likelihood of being made to suffer for it later if they chose incorrectly. Indeed, those who chose the wrong side even now had to answer for it – any who came out in favour of the King while living in a "liberated zone" risked beatings, bricks through windows, and arson attacks. The same was true of those in a militarised zone who voiced support for the partisans – though cases were not as common, the soldiers themselves being forbidden from harassing civilians.

Many, if not most, civilians left their homes rather than be involved even passively in the conflict, resulting in the greatest refugee crisis Britain had ever experienced. Many of those from long-established families had relatives or friends in smaller towns who would accommodate them. But a family of first-generation immigrants typically would not have that option, and found its only accommodation to be a tent in a farmer's field outside the city.

It only became a crisis when the fields were suddenly – and literally – swamped. Rain, caravans, hundreds of vehicles, thousands of tents, and tens of thousands of feet, turned the refugee camps into quagmires dwarfing the largest and most disastrous music festivals.

Some farmers dealt kindly with the refugees, providing them with sundry assistance according to their ability, while others resented the intrusion and did whatever they could to make the outcasts' lives more difficult.

The Red Cross and other international charities offered help, providing water and food, sanitary and sanitation facilities, and putting relatives in contact with one another, but the crisis remained a crisis.

News services around the world reported on the humanitarian tragedy in Great Britain, comparing it to the mass exoduses of Rwanda, Zimbabwe, Mali, Somalia, and Syria. There were suggestions that international intervention, possibly military, would be forthcoming if the British government did not get a handle on the situation. One news service even reported that the United Nations were considering sending peacekeeping forces to Britain, though this was widely considered to be a fabrication by a less-than-reputable Internet news service.

The general consensus and the advice being given to the Princess was, if the Crown and the military were not willing to decimate more cities, the insurgent threat would not go away.

Meeting with the Princess were General Montgomery, Prime Minister Hollings, Admiral of the Fleet Fredrick Billington, Commandant General of the Royal Marines Major-General Owen Fleetwood, and Air Chief Marshal Sir Jacob Waring of the Royal Air Force. Olivia Trafford acted as stenographer.

"That is certainly not my first choice," Princess Frances said. The conference was being held in one of Buckingham Palace's dining rooms, the table being more than large enough to host them all. Tea and coffee were provided in a china service, together with jugs of water and glasses, many of which stood half-empty in front of the delegates. "I don't want to go down in history as the decimator of Britain's cities. The last one who had that honour was Adolf Hitler. And even if it could be done with only enemy lives lost, the cost of rebuilding… well, York alone will cost a king's ransom."

"Then it's time we truly got serious about killing the enemy." General Montgomery looked at each delegate in turn, and then at the Princess, with grave eyes. "If not by the same methods that were used in York, then by other methods. Perhaps snipers on the rooftops…"

"Can you snipe forty thousand of them?" Admiral Billington looked at the General, eyes wide, hands pleading. "Don't forget, they have a tendency to hide. And besides, the police have snipers as well."

"Sleeping gas, perhaps? Then move in and mop up…"

"Mmm, perhaps. However, it's not hard to get away from the influence of gas – or can you blanket the entire city in it? And how long does it last? Would there be time enough to 'mop up'?"

"Very well," the Princess said, putting her hands palms-down on the table. "Look into it. Consider any other options as well. However, any proposed solution is to come through me for approval or rejection. Now, thank you all for attending. Good day. General Montgomery – please stay a moment."

The delegates took their leave, and only the Princess, Montgomery, and the stenographer remained.

"You may go as well, Miss Trafford." In a moment they were alone. "Now Stewart, I need you to put a team together. Ghosts – people who can enter a situation, deal with it, and get out without the enemy ever knowing that they were there. They need to be able to think on their feet, and kill without compunction. They also must take their orders directly from myself. Whatever they do for me, I will take the blame, or the credit. Can you give me such a team?"

"Of course, Your Highness. But why under your command? I mean no disrespect, but you have no experience commanding a military unit. Just tell me what mission you want accomplished, and I'll find the right man to command it, an experienced field operative."

"Stewart, I respect your reservations. We haven't been working together for very long, but I believe that in time – if my father remains out of the picture – you will come to respect my judgement. Now, can you provide what I've asked or not? Or should I ask the Marines?"

A four-seater economy car drove into Droylsden, in the suburbs of Manchester. The car lit up the darkened streets with its headlights, finding little competition for space on the roads.

Four men rode in the car, each sporting a short haircut, and each similarly attired in a warm coat, dark soft trousers, and running shoes.

None of the men smiled or spoke, and each one's face was a mask of grim determination. Driving the vehicle was Jimmy Bennett. His passengers were Ethan, Mohammed, and Louis.

Driving on through the nondescript streets, they continued until they neared the city centre, turning into a small residential road.

"Any further and we hit a checkpoint." Jimmy stopped the car and set the handbrake.

"And we don't wanna hit a checkpoint," Louis, a freckled white youth with light brown hair, said from the back seat.

"We're packing enough heat to take out a checkpoint," Ethan said, a rough-looking young black man sitting next to Louis.

"Oh yes," Mohammed said from the front, "as if that wouldn't give us away. Don't be thick."

"I'm not havin' no 'paki' tellin' me I'm thick!"

"I'm not a 'paki'. I'm a 'towel head'. Get your terms right."

Ethan slapped Mohammed in the back of the head.

Mohammed turned and attempted to slap Ethan, who dodged and parried despite the cramped space in the back seat.

"C'mon, quit sending each other love-letters. Everyone out." Jimmy set the example by opening his door and getting out, and the other followed his example.

Mohammed offered one more parting slap to Ethan's head before he and Louis removed their coats, revealing black sweatshirts, to which they added black woollen caps.

Jimmy and Ethan opened the car boot and removed two long packs of gear, which they handed to Mohammed and Louis. The freckled white man and the tan-skinned arab accepted the packs and slung them across their backs, fastening the straps diagonally across their chests.

"Okay," Jimmy said, "let's do this." He pressed a finger into his ear, wiggling it about. "Test, one, two. Yeah?"

The others nodded. "Gotcha boss," Ethan said, "loud and clear."

Mohammed and Louis began to climb the wall of a nearby block of flats, ascending rapidly by means of pipes and tiny recesses in the brickwork as hand- and foot-holds.

Jimmy and Ethan set off walking back toward the main road, turning down it to resume their journey on foot.

Soon, visible ahead of them was an army checkpoint. Cars and pedestrians waited in queues as soldiers processed them.

Jimmy and Ethan removed their caps and got in line.

After a few minutes' waiting, it was their turn. Jimmy submitted to being frisked, his rucksack examined, and his identification verified, while glancing furtively up at a rooftop running parallel to the street and glimpsing the black-clad figures of his accomplices making their way along a ledge.

The soldier processing Jimmy began to turn, as if to look at whatever Jimmy had looked at. "Hey," Jimmy said as the guard looked back at him, "can't you go any faster, mate? Things to do, you know!"

"Goin' as fast as I can," the guard said.

Jimmy sneaked another look as Mohammed and Louis pressed themselves into the shadow of an arched window frame.

Again, the guard looked in the direction Jimmy had looked. The other guards, noticing this one looking, also looked.

"C'mon," Ethan said, pushing his way into the guard's space, "it's my go now. You're takin' forever."

The guard's attention turned back to Ethan and Jimmy while his colleagues still looked up at the ledge.

"Get back," the guard said to Ethan, still holding Jimmy's rucksack.

"I said, it's my go now. You still not finished with him?"

"Get back, or I might just take even longer!"

"You wouldn't talk t'me like that if I wasn't black," Ethan said loudly, pushing himself further into the guard's personal space, "would ya?"

Now all the soldiers turned to look at Ethan.

"Bein' court-martialled for racism," the guard said, "is not exactly the worst thing that can happen t'me right now, so back off. Yeah?"

Unobserved, Jimmy saw Mohammed and Louis move on, out of sight.

"Come on mate," Jimmy said, looking at Ethan, "don't be so sensitive! The girls are waitin' an' we don't wanna be late."

Ethan put his chest out and shoulders back, taking a rapid step toward Jimmy. "Sensitive? You talkin' t'me?"

"Here," the guard said, handing Jimmy's rucksack to him. "You," pointing at Ethan, "back off, or I'll turn you back. Now, identification!"

Ethan took a passport out of his pocket and, holding it between his fingers, flicked it like a spent cigarette at the guard. The passport bounced off the guard's chest and landed at his feet. He picked it up and looked it over, then flicked it back to Ethan in the same manner.

"Now, stand here" – the guard pointed to the ground at his feet – "and hold your arms out like this."

"I ain't lettin' you feel me up!" Ethan took a step back, eyes wide, scowling.

"Either I feel you up," the guard said, still pointing at the ground, "or you go back where you came from!" The other guards, glancing over from their own tasks, laughed.

Ethan submitted with a deep sigh, rolling his eyes and sighing some more while the guard frisked him. "Had your fun now?"

The guard pointed impatiently in the direction of the city centre, scowling at Ethan, who did not move right away.

Ethan pointed a tense finger at the guard. "I'm reporting you to your boss!"

"Sorry about my friend," Jimmy said. "I didn't think you were gonna let him through."

"I've had worse than him." The guard turned away, motioning forward his next subject.

Jimmy and Ethan walked away from the checkpoint and toward the city centre.

"If I'd been him," Ethan said, "I wouldn't have let me through."

"Then it's a good thing he ain't you."

"And I gotta say," Ethan said, "I feel a little stupid goin' through an army checkpoint with a fake ID. All we needed to do was show them our army IDs, and we would'a been through in a second, and with our guns."

"Well, if we can fool the army, we can fool the cops."

"Yeah. Famous last words."

"Well, if they're my last words," Jimmy said, "I'm glad they're gonna be famous."

They moved through the entire buffer zone without problems, keeping pace with Mohammed and Louis who were navigating the rooftops with confident parkour.

Soon they came to the city centre – the so-called Liberated Zone – and the police roadblock.

This one was easier than the previous checkpoint, and they were through it in a few minutes.

Mohammed and Louis could not stay on the rooftops, having to climb down and up again several times to cross streets or car parks. Here and there they stayed on ground level, passing behind buildings instead of over them, taking a view of each situation as needed.

Jimmy and Ethan parted ways at a junction, Jimmy continuing on Whitworth Street and Ethan turning left on Princess Street.

At the junction with Oxford Street Jimmy paused, looking at the floodlit structure of the Palace Hotel on his left and the Palace Theatre on his right.

The hotel was an imposing red-brick structure combining classical, gothic, and art-deco styles into Mannchester's most stylish five-star guest house. Downstairs was normally crowded with the city's wealthies or wannabes, while the upper floors offered overnight luxury to those able and willing to pay the high rates.

The theatre was a more modern construction which some considered ugly and others hideous, but was nevertheless host to the biggest shows from the West End and elsewhere.

With the city under what amounted to martial law, neither building currently lived up to its potential, and most of the busyness around them was police and sober civilian traffic.

Turning right on Oxford Street, Jimmy walked the length of the theatre, and the longer building which joined onto it, and went right again, and again, until he found himself in a narrow alley which meandered to a canal, across which was the back of the theatre. Crossing the canal at a lock-gate, he looked up and down the building, approached a large pipe, and began to climb. His progress was slow: he searched for hand- and foot-holds, hoisted himself up, looked down, looked up, and repeated.

When at last he hauled himself over the edge and onto the theatre's roof, Mohammed – now wearing an abseiling harness – was waiting for him, offering a hand.

"How long," Jimmy said, panting, "have you been up here?"

"Long enough to watch you sweat it," Mohammed said. "You are so out of shape."

Jimmy crouched, resting his hands and the weight of his upper body on his bent knees, still breathing heavily.

The roof sloped upward to a peak, which obscured Jimmy's view of the Palace Hotel.

Mohammed moved to where he had left his equipment. A sheet was spread out, on which was one long rifle equipped with a telescopic sight, and another half-assembled with an assortment of parts next to it.

"Now you're here you can finish putting it together," Mohammed said.

Having got his breath back, Jimmy put his woollen cap on and moved across the roof in a hunched posture, kneeling beside the half-assembled rifle. His hands moved quickly to complete the assembly, including a shoulder strap. When he had finished he put on a harness like Mohammed's.

Already lying prone at the peak of the sloped roof, Mohammed was holding his weapon in sniping position as he looked through the 'scope, not in the direction of the hotel, but another rooftop on the opposite corner of the junction. He took one hand off the rifle and waved subtly.

Jimmy joined him and looked down his own rifle's sights at the building diagonally across the junction, to see Louis and Ethan looking back at him through their rifles' sights, and gave a tired wave. They were taking cover behind the low wall which ran along the rim of the flat roof. "Okay, never mind the greetings." Ethan shrugged and turned his rifle. Jimmy looked at his companion. "Any sign of the mark?"

"Not yet." Mohammed moved his sights back to the hotel. "The lights are off."

"Top floor, first five windows," Jimmy said, turning his own gun on the hotel. The top corner of the hotel was topped by a decorative turret with a living space inside. Two of the windows were in the turret, and three in the straight wall. The other angle of this corner would be visible to Louis and Ethan.

"Yep, lights are off. Well, it's still early." Jimmy put a finger to his ear. "Quit moaning. Got something better to be doing at this hour?"

"You talkin' to me?" Mohammed said.

"Them," Jimmy said, glancing toward their counterparts on the other roof. "Put your earpiece back in."

"It distracts me. I need to focus."

Jimmy sighed and resumed watching the hotel. "It distracts him. He needs to focus."

Mohammed ignored the words, giving all his attention to the five darkened windows.

Jimmy got up and, staying low, went to the back edge of the roof and attached a climbing rope to a protruding ventilation fixture, coiled the rope, and left it resting at the edge. He returned to his position.

One hour later, the sun rose.

Another hour later, the lights came on.

Mohammed had scarcely moved at all.

Jimmy stretched his arms, yawning. "Movement?"

"Not yet. Ah! There!"

Regaining his grip on the rifle, Jimmy scanned the five windows with his 'scope. "Oh yes," he said.

Sir Patrick Blackwell-MacIntyre walked across the space of the five narrow windows to stand in the turret, looking out toward Jimmy and Mohammed.

They pressed themselves under the level of the roof's peak, out of Sir Patrick's view.

"Have you got a shot?" Jimmy said. "Then take it."

There was a quick succession of 'pop' sounds accompanied by the breaking of glass.

Looking over the roof's peak again, Jimmy could no longer see Sir Patrick, but there was a spatter of blood on the glass where Sir Patrick had been.

"Is the target down?" Jimmy listened. "Okay, move out. See you back at HQ, I hope."

A commotion of voices began to rise up from street level.

Mohammed had already slung his rifle, the strap crossing his chest diagonally, while the rifle rested against his back, and he was now fitting his earpiece. Jimmy slung his weapon as well, and they traversed the roof to the rope.

Mohammed picked up the coil and tossed it over the side, holding the end of it and shaking it out. He clipped the rope through the carabiners on his harness and jumped over the side, abseiling to the ground in a few seconds.

Jimmy followed, but Mohammed was way ahead of him. By the time Jimmy had crossed the canal, a matter of another few seconds, the darker man was nowhere to be seen.

He ran like a olympic sprinter along the alleys, emerging onto a road, without slowing down, staying away from the main roads, using small alleys and ginnels wherever possible.

Turning to head north-east, he heard commotion of people and vehicles in all directions. He stopped, looking around. There were no people visible, having the little side road to himself.

There were heavy iron grates in the ground, along the edges of the buildings, preventing easy access to basement windows. Jimmy found one such grate which was not fastened, and removed it. He dropped his rifle and black skullcap into the space, then removed and reversed his coat, transforming it from black to a casual light brown.

Taking a deep breath, he exhaled and walked to the end of the road, emerging onto a much wider road. In the distance was a militia checkpoint. He walked on toward it, searching in his pockets, removing his papers, examining them, and ignoring all the comings and goings of police units.

When he arrived at the checkpoint, he was prepared to show his papers. But a sizeable queue had developed, and those waiting in it were protesting and moaning to the uniformed policeman acting as border guards.

"It's no good whingeing to me," the cop nearest to Jimmy said, shouting and holding his arms up for silence. "We can't let anyone else through till the alert's over."

Some of those in the queue demanded to know what was going on.

"Don't you worry about that. Just go back to your homes and try again later."

"But my home is on the other side," someone said, pointing to the militarised zone.

"Not my problem, mate. Go get yourself some breakfast, and maybe it'll have blown over when you come back."

"Breakfast? Where? Nothing's open since your lot moved in!"

Jimmy turned around, going back the way he had come.

Princess Frances and General Montgomery sat at the conference/dining table, with Miss Trafford at the opposite end writing in her notebook.

"Yes, Mr Denham," the General said, looking at the centre of the table, "your information was extremely helpful, as I'm sure you already know. Your first clue would surely have been Patrick Blackwell-MacIntyre lying dead on his hotel room floor from a sniper's bullet. To be perfectly frank, Mr Denham, I have my reservations about someone who can betray his own leader to death the way you did. Why did you sell him out this way? Not that I'm not glad you did, only that I'm concerned about your character and how far we can trust you."

The owner of the voice on the other end of the line cleared his throat. "General, I was never under any delusions as to what the result would be. I always respected Sir

Patrick… but what else could I have done? How many more men on both sides would have been killed? How many more cities rendered uninhabitable? Sir Patrick had gone completely off the deep end. There was no other choice. I'm not happy about what I did, but nor do I regret it."

"You're absolutely right, Mr Denham," the Princess said. "Your information has saved many lives, and much of our urban heritage. In fact, I'm tempted to give you a knighthood."

"No. Definitely not. That would destroy my credibility utterly."

"I understand that, Mr Denham. But you've no idea how pleased I am that we can avoid further bloodshed and destruction."

"I think I have some idea, Your Highness. This conflict was never going to be any good, for you, or for my members. And by the way, please call me Chester. Now, may we discuss returning control of the cities to you, and a general amnesty for my members?"

"There cannot possibly be any amnesty," Montgomery said, "for any of your members who killed any of our soldiers."

"I can appreciate that General," Chester said, "but how do you propose to differentiate those who killed and those who did not?"

General Montgomery took a breath and opened his mouth, but Princess Frances spoke first. "That's a question that will require further discussion. But in principle, I agree with the General. I expect there will be comparatively few who'll not be able to benefit from an amnesty. In the meantime, you may start by dismantling your security checkpoints. We still have two men unaccounted for in Manchester."

"They never asked for clearance," the RAF air traffic controller said to her superior officer. "They just showed up."

The officer leaned in close over the controller's shoulder, adjusting his glasses as he peered at the display. "That's an American call-sign all right."

"That's what I've been saying, Sir."

"How extraordinary. The Americans are actually violating our airspace. I'll have to send this upstairs. Well done, controller. Glad you've kept your wits about you."

"You mean, like, not shot it down, sir? You're welcome. I just didn't want to be the one to start world war three. Not today, at least."

"I hope not," the officer said, smiling. "I think Jamison over their is bucking for that honour."

The controller and the officer looked over at a young man manning yet another radar screen. He gave a thumbs-up signal without looking away from his screen or interrupting his communication through his headset.

Taking a pad from the controller's station, the officer wrote down the aircraft's call-sign and position, and tore the sheet off. "Right, I'll go and see what the brass want to do about this. Meantime, you keep hailing."

"I will," she said, "but so far they've kept radio silence for as long as I've had them on the scope."

"I see. Very well. Carry on."

The officer left the control tower.

Captain Richard "Dickie" Roberts was asleep in his bunk when the first torpedo hit his ship.

Instantly awake, Roberts ran to his desk and punched the intercom. "Commander, was that what I thought it was?"

"Please come to the bridge, sir," Commander Indrani said, her voice crackling over the intercom. "We are under attack."

"On my way!"

Dressed in his pyjamas, the Captain opened his wardrobe and began to select a uniform. But as their engines laboured and the ship lurched, the Captain abandoned the wardrobe and selected his dressing gown instead, putting his arms through the sleeves while slipping his feet into his slippers. He hit the button and as the door slid aside with a hydraulic hiss the Captain stumbled into the corridor, swaying with the increased motion of the ship as he tied off his belt.

A moment later he was on the bridge. The crew wore orange lifejackets and were engaged in a flurry of activity as they manned battle stations.

Commander Indrani stepped forward and saluted. "Captain! They fired only one torpedo, but managed to knock our starboard screw out of commission. That's why we're going round in circles, but I thought it was better than standing still. You know, moving target and all that."

"Well done, Commander," Roberts said, as a crew member came up behind him and helped him on with a lifejacket. "But who did this? Who fired a torpedo at us?"

"You're not going to believe this sir," Indrani said, "but it was the Americans."

"What? You're kidding!"

"I wish I was, Sir."

"That's why you didn't fire back."

"Yes sir. I mean, no sir. It'd be World War three."

"Have they said anything?"

"Just that they wanted to speak to the Captain. Are you ready to talk to them?"

"Yes, Commander. Open a channel. And fast!"

It was done in a moment.

An American voice sounded clearly over the speakers. "Hello Dickie. Long time no see. Is everyone okay over there?"

A scowl of recognition crept over Captain Roberts's face. "Chuck? Was that you hurling torpedoes at us? What're you playing at?"

"Yes, it's Captain Maguire here. And yes, it was our torpedo. Sorry about that."

"You've come a long way since our joint Anglo-American manoeuvres. You mind telling me what's going on?"

"Calm down, buddy," Maguire said over the radio. "I'm only following orders here. Now, you're leaking fuel fast. Stop your remaining engine so the Seattle can come alongside and evac your crew."

"Stop being so jocular, Chuck. Two of my seamen were killed when you took a pot-shot at us. And it could have been a lot worse if it'd been daytime."

"I'm…" Maguire paused. "I am sorry about that, Dickie. I mean it. I really am. But, like I said, I had my orders. And my ongoing orders are to take you and your ship. Now, please, stop your remaining engine, and let us board you."

"Or I could return fire."

"You really don't want to do that, Dickie. You're out here all by yourself."

Roberts looked enquiringly at Indrani. She held up a hand, extending all her fingers, and mouthed the words, "five ships".

"Okay. You win, Chuck. We're your prisoners."

"No, Dickie. Think of yourselves as our guests."

"They're circling us like vultures, Your Highness," Admiral Billington said as he walked alongside Princess Frances and General Montgomery, keeping a brisk pace through the corridors and hallways of Buckingham Palace, "forming a blockade around our west coast and Scotland."

"How can they spare that many ships?" the General said.

"The US Navy is quite large, you know," the Admiral said. "The ships are spaced quite generously, but there are still a lot of them. And it's not only the United States."

Montgomery raised an eyebrow. "No?"

The men moved aside to let some others pass, while the Princess continued forward, forcing those coming toward her to manoeuvre around her.

"No. France has deployed most of her navy to help them."

"Oh," the Princess said, smoothing the fabric of her Harris tweed suit with her hands, "this is intolerable! Have any of their ships crossed into our waters?"

"Not yet. But after the Dominance, I don't think that matters. Firing on one of our ships, unprovoked, is just as much a hostile act as violating our waters."

"Yes." She paused speaking but walked more briskly. "Right. Bring all our surface ships home. Does that meet with your approval, Admiral?"

"Yes and no. I'd like them safe, but that's not what ships are made for."

"So what would you advise, Frederick?"

"With our ships spread around the world, the fuel cost alone of bringing them home would be difficult to bear. At any time now, the countries we buy oil from might cut us off. We need to be very careful. I say we keep the ships where they are for now, only group them so none are on their own."

"Good. Do that. Now, what about the airspace violations?"

"Ah, that's been becoming more frequent," Montgomery said, "almost as if they're goading us. The RAF – and your boys as well, Frederick – are just itching to start firing at them. Obviously we're not doing that. We don't want to be the ones who get blamed for starting an Anglo-American war."

"I don't want it to happen in any case," Frances said, "regardless who'd take the blame."

"Neither do I," Admiral Billington said. "Unless we can win."

"They are much bigger than we are," Montgomery said.

"Yes... but smaller and less well-equipped countries have held their own against the Americans before."

"Let us simply," the Princess said with a cutting gesture, "rule out that option. First, I will see what the Ambassador has to say. Then we'll know what our options are. Now get to work."

Arriving at her father's office, Frances opened the door and stepped inside, leaving the General and Admiral to continue on their ways.

Ambassador Stapleton sat on a chair at the coffee table, while Miss Trafford poured coffee for him from a china pot.

Stapleton stood. "Good morning, Your Highness. It's good to see you again."

"I wish I could say the same. To either sentiment." She took a seat across from Stapleton. Miss Trafford poured her a tea.

"I sympathise with your feelings, Your Highness. But please try to–"

"I do not believe you sympathise. My feelings run the gamut from betrayal all the way to hatred. And when our closest ally declares war on us, my feelings are fully justified."

He raised his hands in protest. "Please Your Highness. There's no question of war being declared."

"In a way, that's disappointing. At least a war would bring clarity. How, then, do you explain the crippling of one of my ships and the capture of its crew?"

"I would say – off the record – that the explanation will depend upon what happens next." A lock of hair once again fell over Stapleton's forehead. "If the President feels that Britain is co-operating then the explanation will be: the torpedo was fired accidentally, and Captain Maguire offered all assistance by evacuating the crew for their safety. If, however, the President feels he's not getting what he wants from you, then we will offer a somewhat different explanation. It can all be retconned, redacted, or rebooted as required." He ran his hand backward through his hair, pushing the lock into place again.

"And why should this be necessary?" Frances folded her hands together in her lap, and held her head up condescendingly. "Exactly what lesson does the President mean to teach us?"

"The 'lesson', if that's what we're to call it, is not primarily for you. There can be no more rogue monarchies. The United States – the President, that is – must discourage any other nations from going down the path Britain is following."

"As you successfully discouraged communism during the Cold War? As I recall, the more sanctions you imposed on communist countries, the more of them sprang up. Perhaps the reality is that America is jealous because they don't have a monarch. Or perhaps the president is jealous because he's not a king."

Stapleton sighed. "Now that's a frivolous suggestion."

"Perhaps. But I did what you wanted. The civil war concerned you, and I ended it. If you're not– excuse me, if your President is not going to consider that in our favour, then what can be done?"

"I'm sorry Your Highness, but it seems to have been too little too late. Who's to say a rebellion won't break out again?"

"The police union, AS-ONE, was led by a madman," she said. "They won't be banding together that way again, for all sorts of reasons."

"Well, at the end of the day – and still off the record," – he looked at Miss Trafford, holding up a warning finger – "and I'm sorry I have to say this – I'm personally convinced Washington intended to do this in any case. Call it unfinished business from 1812. There are those within the establishment even now who want to settle that finally. Or call it making an example of you – in which case there's not much you can do to stop it. As an excuse, requiring you to stop the civil war was convenient, but we din't actually need it." The Ambassador leaned forward in his chair. "We're Americans."

"Back on the record then, what does the President want of us?"

Stapleton looked at Miss Trafford, then back at the Princess, holding her eye. "He wants you to give up the monarchy. Restore Parliament and democracy."

"Come now, Edward, there must be another way."

"Off the record again, yes there is." He drew a deep breath, holding it for a long moment. "War."

Captain Roberts was being held with some of his crew in a large multi-purpose room onboard the USS Seattle, while the rest of the Dominance's crew had been split up and taken into custody on several ships, segregated by sex.

There were tables, chairs, and several temporary cots, though still some had to sit on the floor.

Roberts stood by a porthole, looking out. His ship was visible about five hundred metres away.

"A bit of a mystery really," Lieutenant Oldfield said. "Do they actually want our ship?"

"It's possible," Roberts said, "though it's hard to imagine why. But it doesn't make a lot of sense to cripple the ship and then steal it. Unless there's something about it we don't know. Some cargo perhaps, smuggled on board?"

Oldfield was covered with a sheen of sweat, as were all the other sailors in the improvised brig. His tie was loosened, and his top button undone, revealing chest hair that came all the way up to his neck. "Maybe they're on some kind of scrap metal drive."

The Captain chuckled quietly, then stiffened, looking down at the expense of water between the Seattle and the Dominance.

"What's that?" Roberts said, looking at a rise in the water moving toward the Dominance, leaving a slight foam in its wake.

The disturbance moved close to his ship.

"No!" Roberts's eyes were wide, teeth clenched.

A crump, a splash, a plume of smoke, and a ball of orange fire erupted from the water level of the Dominance, where the trail of the disturbance ended.

It was quickly followed by another explosion, which sent fire and debris blasting from the ship.

As some of the smoke cleared, two great holes became visible, the metal hull layers peeled and torn like an orange's skin.

Striking the farthest end of the crippled ship this time, further torpedo ripped a third breach.

The Dominance was taking on water, filling up and sinking fast.

Captain Roberts watched, transfixed, as his ship slowly disappeared under the roiling water surrounded by the otherwise serene ocean, clenching his teeth and gripping the rim of the porthole so his knuckles were white.

In a few moments, the only visible evidence that a ship had ever been there was a patch of white water.

Releasing his hand from the porthole with an effort, the Captain staggered over to one of the chairs, which a rating vacated for him, and slumped into it.

Holding his hands out to the Captain as if trying to decide whether to offer any assistance, Lieutenant Oldfield sat down next to the him.

Roberts assumed a crouch, resting his forehead on his hands, eyes to the ground. He visibly shuddered as he gulped the air.

The door opened. The Captain and the Lieutenant, together with everyone else in the room, looked.

Captain Maguire entered, flanked by a detachment of six military police armed with standard light assault weapons.

To a man, the crew members of the late HMS Dominance scowled at Captain Maguire and his armed retinue.

"What is the meaning," Roberts said, standing up and moving forward to face Maguire, "of this outrage?"

"Sorry Dickie," McGuire said, rubbing his chin with his large mitt of a hand. "The Dominance seems to have sunk. It was obviously more badly damaged than we thought."

Roberts's lip curled into a half sneer. "It is now, that's for certain."

"Now Dickie," McGuire said as he began to slowly walk around the area, "try not to be so upset. You've been floating around in that twenty-five-year-old tub for how long now? It was due to be replaced in the next few years anyway. This little 'accident' has done you a favour."

"Incident," Roberts said, his sneer softening not at all, "not accident."

"I understand the official story is yet to be decided on." McGuire stopped walking and took a stance facing Roberts. "One thing's for sure: it's not be decided at our level. This is a matter for nations, not Captains."

7

Edge

Blair Lindsey sat at a small table in a corner, poring over his notebook as he transcribed his neat shorthand into the tablet computer in front of him.

Spreading out around him, the situation room was abuzz with activity. Uniformed representatives of all the armed services and dark suited men and women busily conferred with one another, some in hushed tones, some with raised voices. Some were hunched over the digital map table, others over computer screens, others gazing at their large tactical display on the wall, and one or two brandishing sheaves of papers.

In an instant, the sound faded and the room was silent. All eyes turned to the door.

"Blair, tell General Montgomery I wish to see him," King Alfred said, his gaunt figure framed in the doorway. Cleaned up and dressed in his customary suit, though now sporting a well-trimmed beard, he nevertheless looked as though his days of starved isolation had taken their toll. "And join me in my office as soon as you've finished what you're doing." He looked around, surveying the crowded room. "Good morning gentlemen, ladies."

As a unit, they replied. "Good morning, Your Majesty."

"Now carry on," the King said with a slightly raspy hoarseness. "You're doing important work." He turned and left the room.

Lindsey made haste to finish off his transcription – stopping long enough to ring the General's assistant and give him the King's message – then stood up, took his notebook, and left the room while tightening his tie.

Arriving at the King's office, he knocked on the door.

"Come!" King Alfred's rich voice said, not shouting but readily audible through the closed door.

Lindsey entered.

The Princess was busy gathering up her things from her father's desk, while he waited with strained patience as Miss Trafford accepted the various paraphernalia from her employer.

"–and since my office is at Kensington Palace," she was saying, "it made sense for me to set up shop here, so to speak, until you were better."

Miss Trafford, her arms full, made an awkward attempt to curtsey to the King, and left the room while Lindsey held the door for her.

Frances carried the remainder of her belongings, smiling at her father. "I've been trying to keep things together while you were indisposed, but it's lovely to see you back on your feet. I'll see you later, father." She moved close to Alfred and leaned close, standing on her toes to kiss him on the cheek.

Turning to the door, the Princess cast a withering look at Lindsey.

"Your Highness, would you like me to bring your things to you? They look heavy."

"Don't worry about me, Mr Lindsey. I've got muscles of my own. See you later, father."

Closing the door behind her, Lindsey turned to the King, who was taking his customary seat. "I concur with Her Highness. It's good to see you back, sir."

"Well, I might've taken more time off if my daughter hadn't got us into a war with America."

"With respect, Your Majesty, I don't think she was the cause."

"No." The King opened a drawer and extracted a small mirror. He looked his face over. "Do you think I look well?"

"Well?" Lindsey ran his fingers over his smooth chin. "Well, you don't look unwell, Your Majesty."

"Hmm. Tactful."

"Honest."

"No doubt about it, Blair, that's a quality of yours I find refreshing. Now, where's my General?"

A knock came at the door.

"Ah. That would be him now, I'll wager."

Lindsey opened the door and Montgomery entered.

The General bowed to his King, and took the seat Lindsey offered. Lindsey then took a seat as well, in an unobtrusive corner.

"Your Majesty–"

"No pleasantries, Stewart. Situation report."

"Of course, sir." Montgomery explained everything that had happened militarily since the King's self-imposed confinement.

Alfred listened with rapt attention.

"And of course, one of the other beneficial effects of the end of the civil… incursion is that all the refugees have gone home – where those homes still exist. Naturally, the farmers will be glad to have their fields back. The Red Cross begin the cleanup operation tomorrow, dismantling the tents and the facilities. In a week you'll never know anyone was there."

"Stop them," Alfred said, holding up his hand as if to halt traffic. "I have the feeling we're going to need those camps again."

"You want the army to interfere with the Red Cross? Why ever for?"

"Have you not yet learned to trust me, Stewart?"

"Your Majesty, you have only just reemerged from several weeks of unexplained disappearance, cutting off contact with all those who trust and rely upon you, during a time of national crisis. Trust must be earned. And sometimes re-earned."

"Well, in any case… a most comprehensive summing-up of the situation, Stewart."

"Thank you, sir." The General looked away, as if distracted. "I must say, though, I never expected the Americans to… well, it came as something of a surprise."

"No. No surprise."

The General resumed eye contact with the King. "I beg your pardon?"

"Come now, Stewart. This trouble has been brewing for two hundred years."

Montgomery cocked his head slightly, raising an eyebrow. "Excuse me?"

"It's quite simple. The War of 1812. It represents unfinished business between Britain and the United States."

"That's an extraordinary theory, Your Majesty, though I don't think it would be wise to base any foreign policy on it."

"It seems to me that our foreign policy is even now being based on it by default. How is it that you seem so surprised by these developments?"

"Britain at war with the United States? Surely it's inherently surprising." Montgomery's eyes narrowed as he surveyed the King's face. "You're not implying you foresaw this?"

"Well…" A faint shadow of a knowing smile dawned on Alfred's face, and quickly faded. "It isn't exactly a bolt from the blue. It has, however, happened rather sooner than I might have expected. I wonder what precipitated our American cousins' involvement?"

"I think," the General said, taking each word slowly, "your absence appears to have precipitated things. The ambassador – and, by extension, the President – has been asking to see you, repeatedly and forcefully."

"Ah." The King closed his eyes and leaned back in his chair. "My daughter did try to tell me. But…"

"There is no 'but', Your Majesty. Your grief was – and is – terrible. The loss of your son… it was just too much of a coincidence. Or…" Montgomery adjusted his posture uncomfortably. "You didn't foresee that as well?"

Alfred sighed, a long, lung-emptying sigh – and took a noticeable moment to resume his breath, which rasped with an asthmatic quality. "I should have." He rubbed his eyes with the heels of his hands, then looked out into the middle of the room, focussing on nothing. "I should have. I might have saved him, and many others as well."

He leaned back in his chair, the springs in its base creaking with age and strain.

"In the event," Alfred continued, "it was just as well I stayed away as long as I did. It forced America's hand."

Montgomery closed his eyes, put his hands up, and shook his head. "I'm sorry, is that somehow meant to be a good thing?"

"It's vital," the King said in a low tone, almost a hoarse whisper. "The other thing I foresaw – and you should have seen this too – is that my dark-ages version of a sovereign Britain was never going to be acceptable to the Western World, but least of all to the United States. And until America's and Britain's issues are resolved, the New Order can never be secure. The first necessary, unavoidable step was the civil war."

"How," Montgomery said, eyebrows furrowed in consternation, "are our troubles with AS-ONE related to America's grievance with us?"

"I don't know the full story. Let's get Mr Denham in and ask him, shall we?"

"Denham?" The General's face glazed over. He blinked. "Chester Denham?"

"Do you really think," the King said, eyes narrowed to slits as he looked at the General, "that our troubles at home and abroad were mere coincidence?"

"You baffle me sometimes, Your Majesty. But I am glad to be working with you again. Taking orders from the Princess did not seem natural."

"It's merely a question of what you're accustomed to, Stewart. You must admit, Frances did a very good job in my absence."

"I don't know… I suppose she did the best she could with what she had to work with."

"Which was you."

Montgomery half-smiled.

"Now, Stewart, I'll let you get back to your duties. Blair will call you when we've organised a meeting."

"With…?"

"With Mr Denham."

"Ah, yes. Well, thank you for your time, Your Majesty."

The General got up, bowing and backing to the door. Lindsey rose and opened it for him.

Chester Denham sat down in the comfortable leather-upholstered chair in the King's office. He took a cup of tea from Lindsey's hand.

Alfred, sitting on the Edwardian sofa, crossed his legs and sipped his tea.

General Montgomery sat on the other chair, sipping and listening, and Lindsey in his unobtrusive corner, writing with his pen.

They spent a short time discussing the proposed amnesty for the AS-ONE members, the General making his reservations clear, and Denham taking a conciliatory attitude throughout.

Montgomery asked Denham what he knew about any connection between AS-ONE and the United States's current belligerence toward Britain.

He looked from Montgomery to the King. "I'm telling you this, Your Majesty, because I have disavowed violence. After seeing what Sir Patrick did with this knowledge… he wasn't exactly mad, you know. He was a fanatic. He knew he was using his members, and did it willingly. Since he believed in the cause, with the entire force of its history, I don't think he could have done any differently.

"Anyway, how much do you know about the War of 1812? Well, basically, America wanted some land in Canada, and Britain owned it. But we were doing some terrible things, so you could say we didn't deserve to hold on to it. America took issue with the terrible things we were doing, and that plus its desire for territory made it willing to go to war with us. Naturally, we were up for that, even though we were already fighting Napoleon at the time.

"Neither side was winning, and after a few years the war was wearing everyone down. So peace was proposed, and the Treaty of Ghent drawn up. In its fifth to eighth articles it provided for two commissioners to be appointed to finally decide the boundaries between Canada and the United States, which was the dispute the war had been fought over.

"It also made provision for the commissioners to appoint a commission to assist them with the legwork – scouting out the disputed areas, doing paperwork, and so forth. On completion of this work, the commission was supposed to disband, which it did – officially.

"The members of the commission, all Freemasons, grew over the course of their work to distrust and disdain Great Britain institutionally. Specifically, the British Crown.

"The anti-royal sentiment spread quickly within Masonry, creating their own ideological divide within the group – a secret society within a secret society. Republicanism gained traction within British masonry as well, taking hold as an anti-royalist group calling itself 'As One'.

"'As One' members widely infiltrated the public services – especially the police – and formed their own labour union, secretly dedicated to the eventual overthrow of the Crown. The eventual merciless response of the Army – my grudging compliments to you and your men, General – convinced most of us to stand down, with the exception of our leader Sir Patrick.

"In America the movement followed a different course. It continued to find traction within Freemasonry, as well as within the Council on Foreign Relations and the Trilateral Commission. The liberal and libertarian flavour of those organisations proved fertile ground for ideas of republicanism as against the despotic, if benevolent, rule of an absolute monarch. The high profile of its members, including many celebrities, and even the President, eased the transition from ideology to undeclared war.

"In short, they view the War of 1812 as unfinished and undecided. They want closure. For all I know, they want to make Britain, quite literally, the 51st State."

Denham stopped speaking. The men sat in silence for a moment.

"But I thought," the General said, "the CFR as an organisation always had world peace as its objective. Now you're telling us what they really want is war? With us?"

"Oh, they want peace all right. But on their terms, and with them in charge. Their connections with socialism and communism in the past were intended to help them toward those goals, but those came to nothing. Now you've handed them the justification they've always wanted – on a plate."

"But your masters," the King said, "in the CFR will be none too pleased with you telling us all about them, will they?"

"No. I could justify brokering peace with the Crown, on the basis of Sir Patrick's actions and the decimation of York. But they won't accept any justification for my spilling all this to you. I don't know if they know yet, but they will soon, and I'll have to chance the consequences."

"Why, then, are you telling us this," Alfred said, "given the risk to yourself?"

"Because I want peace as well – but on broader terms than they do."

"Peace," Alfred repeated. The men looked at one another. For a moment, their breath and the ticking clock were the only sounds. "Well, since we all want the same thing, shall we finish the meeting on that note?"

They all stood up.

Lindsey opened the door for Denham, and a waiting soldier escorted the AS-ONE chief away.

"Stewart, detail the SIS to put an armed shadow on Chester," the King said as he sat down. "I don't want anything to happen to him."

"Of course, Your Majesty."

Alfred drummed his fingers on the desktop. "Now, what do we do with this new information, hmm?"

"Father, why wasn't I invited to that meeting?" Princess Frances faced the King, her eyes flashing anger. "I ran the country while you were away. I know what's what. I need to keep my hand in."

She forced a brilliant smile as another guest arrived, approaching the King, and then the Princess, to shake their hands. Standing just inside the door, father and daughter received their guests with outward grace, directing them to the sumptuously appointed dinner table in the centre of Buckingham Palace's impressive dining room.

The guest moved on, and Frances resumed her angry demeanour.

"You can read the minutes," Alfred said, "when Blair has finished with them. But why should you want to? You were never interested in matters of State before."

The smiles reappeared on their faces as Archbishop Youngblood approached them, arm in arm with his icily attractive wife. "Janice, my favourite niece, it's so good to see you. And you, Woollie." Alfred shook the clergyman's hand with a firm grip.

Youngblood returned the King's smile. "Thank you, Your Majesty. I trust you are doing as well as can be expected." He looked at the Princess. "And you, Your Highness. It must be good to be out of the driving seat again."

"Oh, definitely, Uncle Woollie. Who needs the responsibility?" Frances flashed a vacuous smile.

The Archbishop moved on, out of earshot.

"I was never a princess in a real kingdom before, father. Now… what if something hap– something else happens to you? If not me, who else is going to look after things, now that it's only the two of us?"

The King took her small hand in his large one, squeezing it. "You just look after yourself. Don't worry about me." His voice was gruff but comforting. "Ah, the guest of honour."

Ambassador Stapleton entered, a young woman of model-quality, at least twenty years his junior, on his arm. The King shook both of their hands warmly.

"My dear Mr Stapleton, I am so glad you were able to spare the time to join us."

"How can I refuse? I'm in your country under sufferance as it is, aren't I? I assume this is going to be a working dinner."

"Never," Alfred said with a lilt of childish innocence. "Well... perhaps a little. Find your place, and we'll get started."

The seating plan placed Youngblood on the King's left, and Stapleton on his right.

Regaling all those in attendance with politely entertaining banter for a few minutes, the King then turned his attention to Ambassador Stapleton.

"Very well Edward, you could not wait for me. You pressured me out of my grief, and gave my daughter the worst possible few days of her short regency. Your country's actions suggest there is something you want. So, what is it? Let the negotiation begin."

"I trust you understand, Your Majesty," the Ambassador said, brushing a comma of hair from his forehead with one hand, while checking the alignment of his tie with the other, "that I'm only a middleman, and as such my power to make decisions on behalf of my President is limited."

"And I trust that you will convey our discussions to your President with my compliments. I'm sure you and he would both concur that our nations would have much more to gain by pooling our resources."

"Forgive me, Your Majesty, if I sound a trifle childish when I say this." A thin serving girl reached over his shoulder and set his first course in front of him in a graceful motion. Stapleton looked at the dish, reached halfway for his fork, drew his hand back. He looked the King in the eye, expressionless. "We have more resources than you. Many more – and much more."

Alfred held Stapleton's eye for a moment, then looked down at his own starter. He took his knife and fork and cut across the thinly sliced rare roast beef, putting a bite into his mouth with a dab of horseradish, and chewed with gentility.

"There's the American arrogance for you," Youngblood said, leaning close to the King and speaking in a low voice, though still loud enough to be overheard by the ambassador. "'Mine is bigger than yours.' Typical."

Alfred swallowed his food and waved a silencing hand at the Archbishop, looking at Stapleton. "We do have some resources ourselves, my dear Edward. Our universities lead the way in technical research. Our scientific boffins are the leaders in their fields, and always have been. We did crack the Enigma code, you know."

"We," Stapleton said, cutting his meat, "have got Apple, Microsoft, and Google." He put a bite into his mouth with a flourish, causing his unruly lock of hair to fall over his forehead again.

The serving maids hovered around the table, keeping wine and water glasses topped up.

The King frowned, scratched at his salty beard, and drank deeply from his wine.

"And now," the Archbishop whispered conspiratorially, "America brandishes its technological hegemony in our faces."

Alfred shushed Youngblood and turned back to Stapleton. "Think of Oxford and Cambridge. Many of your best people have been educated there. Even one of your presidents. And consider our museums. The British Museum and the British library have some of the finest collections in the world. And then there are the National Gallery, the Tate, and many others, not to mention my own private collection, and those of many other British collectors. All of these have lent a wealth of items to your museums."

"And we have humoured you by accepting them," the Ambassador said, pushing the hair back from his forehead. "Our Metropolitan Museum, Guggenheim collections, Smithsonian… more than enough for our needs. And we've got the Ivy League. We certainly don't need Oxbridge."

"You see, Your Majesty?" Youngblood looked daggers at the Ambassador, as he whispered semi-privately to the King. "Complete philistines, these Americans."

The King looked past the ambassador, and then made eye contact with him. "There must–" His voice came out gravelly. He took a drink of water, and turned his attention to his plate, cutting another bite and putting it in his mouth. He chewed rapidly, frowning.

Looking back at Stapleton, the King spoke. "What do we have that the United States want?" His angry eyes almost pleaded with the Ambassador.

"Nothing." Stapleton set his cutlery down on his empty plate.

Alfred put his cutlery down and leaned back in his chair, though his plate was not empty.

Youngblood leaned forward, resting his elbows on the table and turning his head to look directly at Stapleton. "You haven't exactly mastered the subtle art of negotiation, have you Ambassador?" He reclined, looked at his plate, crossed his arms. "Or perhaps you're just too subtle."

"Ambassador Stapleton– Edward," Alfred said through clenched teeth, "what do you– what does the United States expect me to do to avoid war?"

"War is such an ugly word, Your Majesty. What else could we call it? Sanctions? Hostilities? The way to avoid them is really quite simple: surrender your claim as ruler of the United Kingdom."

The King pressed his quivering lips together, his brow furrowing, his jaw muscles knotting. He clenched his fists and brought them crashing down on the table with a noise that drew everyone's attention and caused one of the serving maids to drop her tray, shattering a tea service.

"How dare you," Alfred shouted, "arrogate to your petulant country authority over the King of Great Britain!" He continued in a moderated tone, which sounded as if it might rise to a crescendo at an instant. "America! You are a mere babe in arms next to us. We were ruling the world while your country was at our breast!" The King leaned ever closer to Stapleton, until he was almost nose-to-nose with him. "My claim to the throne of United Kingdom has greater validity than your President's claim to his."

Stapleton's face was beaded with sweat. He was trying to speak, but no words came.

All eyes were upon Alfred. He stood up, sending his chair clattering over behind him, where a serving girl jumped out of the way. He extended his arm, pointing to the door. "Leave us."

"Your Majesty, I–"

"Get out! Now!" The King quaked with apoplexy.

Stapleton, stood up, looking around the room at each of the other guests. His gaze fell upon Princess Frances, who met his eyes with a sympathetic aspect, and he departed, a footman opening and closing the door for him.

Frances stood up, dropping her napkin on the table, and followed Stapleton.

Walking briskly along the corridor and flanked by Palace staff, Stapleton was not so much being escorted as leading. His gait was almost a jog, and his mien a frown.

"Edward!" The Princess strode at her best pace, her bodyguard in tow, but Stapleton was getting no closer. "Wait! It wouldn't be proper for me to run."

Stopping, he turned and looked at her with an impatient stance and a comma of hair hanging over his brow.

"Edward, why?" She continued walking until she was in front of the American.

"Your Highness," he said, his voice shaky, "I didn't want any of this. I have been speaking for my country, not for myself. I've been doing my job. That's all. If I had been addressing you, I would have said the same things. I wish – now more than ever – that we were on the same side. My… personal regard for you is unchanged. Would that you were unmarried."

"Ha ha. And that you were British. And aristocracy! You'd have made a good royal. You speak a bit like us already. With a little more coaching, perhaps…"

Smiling, Stapleton began to breathe normally again.

"Perhaps," she said, "you could apply for citizenship here. I know my father likes you, really."

"That would be a 'big ask', as you Brits say. Renouncing one's nationality is no light thing. Anyway, thanks for cheering me up. You go back to your dinner. The main course should just be arriving. I'll go get a Big Mac or something."

"Ah, your true colours shine through. Have a good evening, Edward."

His escort led him away, and the Princess returned to the dining room.

8

Prisoners

All the refugees who had homes to go back to did so, returning to their cities without further apparent threat of battle.

The rest continued to occupy the camp nearest to York, with generous help from the Crown. The King sunk much of his own money into making the camp clean and comfortable for those who had to remain. He had even made a visit to the camp, impressing those who met him by simply being there, given his obvious tiredness and fatigue and the way he attempted to hold back his coughs. He gave the impression of suffering with his subjects, though none mentioned that he would soon be back in his palace.

All the other refugee camps had been closed – but kept intact.

Chain-link fencing topped with razor-wire had been erected around the empty camps, and the facilities cleaned.

Armoured police buses began to arrive at each facility, disgorging cargoes of AS-ONE members, who were then roughly escorted into the camps and held there.

Busload after busload emptied into the camps, which became dangerously overcrowded.

Prison Governors moved in as well, setting up their own camps in well-appointed caravans outside each fenced facility.

Armed guards, either army or non-AS-ONE police, patrolled the perimeter constantly. There was much shouting and internal fighting, but little which seriously worried the guards.

Some of the guards, being veterans of battles on home ground in which AS-ONE forces had shot at them or even killed their friends, could not spare the prisoners any tokens of courtesy, except under the watchful eyes of their commanding officers and the governors. Others were more ready to hope that a new leaf would be turned over by their charges.

With some thirty-thousand offenders to try, an army of pro-bono counsel were recruited – some said compelled – to prepare the cases fully before presenting them to the court-martial judges. A military court was the only framework which could handle such a number of cases in a short time, the civil courts being over-utilised already, as always.

For the most part, the cases were decided in advance. The only extenuating circumstance allowed would be having failed to kill any soldiers in the conflict, which would presumably apply to most of the prisoners. In these cases the only way to establish this would be polygraph tests, since most defendants would presumably claim they hadn't killed anybody whether it was the truth or not. In a few cases there would be witnesses who could be called to back up the lie detector results.

Various shades of guilt would be allowed, such as having fired upon the enemy but not knowing if any hits had been scored, or one having thought he had killed but in reality only injured or missed entirely, or having shot and injured only.

"About half of them, I think," Montgomery said as he watched the King swing his croquet mallet ever so slightly to ease the ball through the hoop. "That, of course, is the whole purpose of a fast-track trial."

"But no sentences have been carried out?" King Alfred moved to where the ball lay, while looking at the General.

"No. They'll all be sorted out at the same time. Some time will have to be allowed for appeals, of course."

"Good."

"Good?"

"Yes, good. I know you're keen to get on with your executions, but–"

"Treason isn't punishable by execution any more, as you know very well, Your Majesty."

Lindsey stood nearby, notebook open and pen in hand, eyes hidden behind a pair of dark sunglasses.

"–but most of them did surrender and present themselves for capture, in the end." Alfred swung his mallet again, and the distinctive crack sounded as it struck the ball, which was sent skittering through another hoop.

"And your point is…?"

"I offered Chester an amnesty. I want to make sure that is kept in mind."

"It is being kept in mind, I assure you. But time is required. Their behaviour in the prison camps affects their eligibility for early release."

"And are your men making it possible for the prisoners to behave themselves?"

"I can't see how they would be making it im-possible. I'm sure you understand there is ill-will on both sides. I have very few men who would be completely impartial. How can a man forget that his prisoners were, only a few days before, shooting at him? No, it won't be easy for them."

"Stewart, you see to it that the prisoners are treated well and fairly, and that they have no excuse not to benefit from the conditions offered to them. I don't want tens of thousands of families broken up if it's possible to avoid it. The negative long-term effects of the civil war will be minimised if the reunions of families can be maximised."

"I'll do what I can."

"I said, see to it, Stewart!"

"Yes, Your Majesty." The General bowed and departed, walking back toward the Palace across the gardens.

"I believe it's your go, Blair."

"Yes sir." Lindsey closed his notebook and set it down on a bench, putting his pen in his inside jacket pocket, before taking a mallet and lining up his shot.

***

Archbishop Youngblood sat, leaning forward in his chair, studying an array of photographs spread across the surface of his desk.

The pictures were of the prison camps, showing the conditions under which the offenders were held at His Majesty'spleasure. There was mud. There were unusually close quarters. There was poor hygiene. There were no activities to occupy the men. There were some candid shots – who knew how they had been captured? – of fights breaking out, of bloodied faces and broken bones. "Is this as bad as it gets?"

Reverend Julian LeBone stood opposite Youngblood's desk. The young Anglican priest wore a full-length black robe, casting him almost in the Catholic mould, except for his short sculpted beard. "Yes sir. But that's pretty bad."

"I've seen worse."

"Probably not in this country."

"Probably not," Youngblood said, frowning as he gazed at a photograph he held in his hand. He looked up at Lebone. "Well, what can we do for these poor men's souls?"

Lebone raised an eyebrow. "That depends on what we want to get back, doesn't it?"

"Mm. I think, to start with, we need to make sure the chaplaincy provision is fully catering to their spiritual needs and human rights."

"Oh, at the very least."

"Let's get our own, hand-picked, chaplains in those camps."

"All of them, sir?"

"Well, we'll start with this one." Youngblood put a finger down on one of the photos.

"That seems about right. And what will be their remit?"

"Well, it looks from these pictures like human rights are a major problem in these camps. Have them start there. The incarcerees need to be aware of their rights. I have the feeling the human rights abuses are only going to get worse as this situation persists."

"I agree completely," LeBone said. "It's possible the soldiers will even receive encouragement in their abuses."

"Well," the Archbishop said through clenched teeth, "so mote it be."

"Then I'd better go look after things – find some reliable men, and so on. With your permission?"

Frowning, Youngblood dismissed LeBone with a wave of his hand, and the young man departed.

Money changed hands, passed down from one to another, its source lost in the chain, until it found its way to a guard.

"The Birmingham Jail," was how the camp in the farmlands outside Birmingham came to be called. It was where the chain ended.

Having pocketed his cash after being told there was more where that came from, Corporal Stanton began his shift. Patrolling the perimeter of the camp, which took a quarter of an hour if one did not stop for any reason, he engaged in conversation with several of the prisoners along the way.

"You look like a killer to me," Stanton said to one of them who had been leaning against the fence, apparently minding his own business.

"Sorry? You talkin' to me?"

"Yeah. You ain't as stupid as you look."

"Oh yeah? You obviously are as stupid as you look. I ain't killed nobody."

"You did! I seen you before – at York. Takin' pot-shots at me mates. Killed one of 'em too! I'll 'ave you for that, just wait."

Stanton raised his rifle butt and stabbed it at the other man's head, who jumped back just in time to avoid being hit. "You're off your head, you are!"

"Right! And you are so dead." Stanton pointed his weapon at the prisoner, who stood transfixed, sweat running down his face.

Other prisoners and guards, seeing what was happening, came near to watch the incident. The prisoners began shouting, taunting and rebuking the soldier. Some other guards came over and forced Stanton's gun down.

The soldiers shouted at the inmates, and inmates at soldiers, while two guards restrained Stanton, who struggled and squirmed out of their grip to brandish his weapon at the inflamed situation.

When enough guards brought their guns to bear, the prisoners stood down and the crowd dispersed. After a token dressing-down by his immediate superior, Stanton resumed his patrol, stopping to taunt several more tough-looking inmates, telling them how he had been just "this close" to shooting one of their worthless number, and begging them to make his day. With the last of these he started another near-riot, and was relieved of his patrol duties with a warning.

The next day, the new chaplains arrived. Euan and Marley, dressed in religious attire, were given specific times they could enter the camp and interact with the inmates, during which they had a mostly free hand to talk to whom they pleased.

"You don't exactly sound like a preacher, padre," a prisoner named Barry said to Reverend Euan, after the vicar had spent some time telling him that he had a right to be treated with dignity.

"Don't I?" Euan said.

"No. You don't talk much about Jesus, or sin, or bein' saved, or that kind'a thing. You know, spiritual stuff."

Euan smiled. "I believe in a social gospel. Let's get your problems sorted out first, then we can think about 'spiritual stuff.'"

"Sure. Whatever you say, padre."

"Good. Then what I want you to know is that you still have rights. Human rights. They can't be taken away from you, whatever your captors might say. You have rights to better facilities, cleaner and more comfortable accommodation, better treatment, time and space for exercise, and so on. You have all the same rights as if you were being held in a proper prison. You need to insist on these things."

"That's easy f'you to say. I'm inside. You ain't. Can't you do somethin' to insist on our rights for us? They might listen to you, but they sure ain't gonna listen to me."

"They will listen to you. They have to if there are enough of you. You have to insist, and keep insisting." Euan held out his hands to the inmate, as if pleading with him. "My colleague and I do what we can, but they don't really listen to us. You men can make a difference. There're so many of you, they can't not listen if you stand together. Organise a protest. Band together."

"An uprising, eh?"

"Yes –" Euan stopped nodding, shaking his head with hands held up in protest. "No! Nothing violent."

"Heh. Sure. You know, I been listenin' to perps demanding their rights for twenty years. Now, here I am doin' the same."

The two chaplains held similar conversations with every prisoner they spoke to, and the responses were usually similar.

"But suppose," Marley said as he gently turned the steering wheel, "they don't take our message to heart? Suppose they decide non-violence isn't the best answer?"

"They're not going to do that. They were police officers, for crying out loud. Surely they joined the police force because they believe in law and order."

The road straightened as it brought them into the outskirts of Birmingham. As they moved through the pools of street lighting, the cat's eyes glinted back the illumination of the car's headlights.

"Haven't you ever heard of police corruption? Police brutality? That sort of thing? Anyway, after what happened, they may not believe in law and order any more."

Euan held up a reassuring hand, which Marley did not see because his eyes were on the road. "There won't be any violence. You think they want to risk their amnesty? No way."

"I expect you're right," Marley said, "but you have to consider the worst-case scenario."

"We've got to trust the Bishop," Euan said, crossing his arms and checking the tension on his seatbelt. "He picked us – and so did the Archbishop – because we're the Church of England's best champions for human rights."

"Hah! That's pretty exalted language for a couple of kids fresh out of seminary."

"Hey, false modesty is just as much of a sin as pride. Anyway, it wasn't my language. That was what The Times said about us, as I know you know."

"So what's your point?"

"My point is that we were chosen for this job because of our particular qualities. So can we just get on with our jobs without agonising over it? I don't just preach social justice, and neither do you. We do social justice. We take the part of the prisoner, the oppressed, the poor, and so on."

"Yes, I do know all that. I'm not arguing with you. I'm on your side."

"Good," Euan said, slapping Marley's knee. "Then enough with the soul-searching already."

Soon they reached their hotel, took to their beds, slept, and returned to the prison camp in the morning to resume their work.

They continued to counsel the prisoners along the same lines. Some of the prisoners even observed that, despite the vicars' occasional forays into psychology and family advice, they were one-issue men: every subject they engaged with always came back to what they were pleased to call human rights.

Continuing in this vein for several days, the chaplains noticed that several prisoners were becoming inflamed against their captors. Asking as to the cause, they were directed toward several of the guards who had been acting and speaking in a provocative manner to the inmates.

***

Stanton and Marley sat opposite one another in a makeshift interview room within a portacabin. A small table stood between them. Euan stood behind his fellow priest.

"Just suppose," Marley said, facing Stanton but looking down and to one side, "the situation had got worse."

"Suppose it had, padre," Stanton said, biting out the religious epithet with contempt. "D'you think I actually feel anything for those cops?"

"You must! They're your fellow men – not to mention Englishmen. They have rights and dignity, which all of us must accord them!"

"They have no rights except what we allow them!" Stanton slammed his fist down on the table, causing it to jump and clatter. "They gave all that up when they turned on us, their country, and their King." He stood up and thrust the table aside with his hand, and it clattered into the wall, its legs folding underneath it. "Your dog collars don't impress me. Under it your neck is still just soft flesh, like everyone else's."

Now red and quaking under the belligerent gaze of the soldier standing over him, Marley closed his mouth tightly while looking up into Stanton's hate-filled eyes.

Euan cleared his throat. "We believe in fair and equal treatment for all. That's why our Bishop sent us here, with your commanding officer's blessing. We're trying to help these men to prepare for re-integration in society, through reconciliation and peace. Can't you see that's a good thing, in all of our interests? Please, stop working against us!"

"You guys are naive as dirt, hiding behind your religion. What d'you know of the real world, hunkering down in your seminaries and cathedrals? You ever been shot at? I have – and by the men in this camp!"

The clergymen stood silently, Marley looking at the floor, and Euan keeping eye contact with the soldier.

Stanton took a step forward. "Don't you try telling me who's got rights."

Marley looked away from the floor and into Stanton's eyes.

"Like it or not, there's amnesty coming," Euan said, his voice cracking and quivering. "You might have to live next door to one of them some day soon."

"Yeah? Well they might be dyin' next door to me," Stanton said, staring into Marley's eyes.

Stanton turned on his heel and left with a brisk, impatient gait.

A guard came in. "Do you want to talk to the next one now?"

Marley put his hands over his face, leaned back, and groaned loudly.

Euan rested his hands and his weight on the back of Marley's chair, looking toward the floor.

"Cheer up, vicars," the guard said, "we're not all as bad as him."

"You lot can rot in there until the end of eternity. You deserve it!" The soldier, brandishing his rifle, stood within an arm's reach of a group of prisoners, the chain-link fence the only buffer between them.

A light rain was adding to the puddles of standing water in the already muddy ground.

Floodlights reflected in the puddles, lighting the area starkly in contrast with the overcast night sky.

Shouts from the assembled prisoners attracted other prisoners and several more guards, facing each other through the diamond mesh of the fence.

None of the voices could be understood clearly now, all shouting at once in both directions. Many soldiers were present, most pointing their guns into the growing crowd of inmates.

Several of the bigger, burlier inmates strutted in front of the others, pushing their chests and chins forward as they shouted taunts and profanities at their captors.

One of the prisoners stopped shouting and wrapped his fingers through the mesh of the fence, pulling at it with all his strength, his digits white and red with the strain. Another joined him, and another, and another, pulling at the fence though it refused to budge.

More men saw what they were doing, and joined in, until ten pulled right, and ten pulled left, heaving with all their might as if they might tear the fence in two.

The interweaved strands of metal bent and stretched slightly, but held intact despite the force being applied to them. Fingers began to bleed and men groaned with effort, while the fence ignored their sweat and blood.

The guards kept their weapons trained on the frenzied inmates, backing away, safeties off, fingers near the triggers. Their gazes darted, from the prisoners, to one another, and back again.

The prisoners gave up their futile attempt to tear the fence, letting go and backing away slightly.

Slowly, most of the guards lowered their weapons, allowing their tense postures to relax. Several had been neglecting to breathe, and now gulped the air afresh.

Then, as one, the prisoners rushed the fence. A combined mass and inertia of possibly a hundred bodies struck it in a concerted moment, and the barrier buckled and crumpled to the ground.

Continuing forward, the men powered through the razor wire, those at the front unable to stop or resist the momentum gathered behind them. Trousers and skin were sliced through, and many caught in the wire fell to be trampled by those surging forward – the thunderous snaps of prisoners' bones breaking underfoot was audible over the commotion of the fevered mob.

Most guards turned and ran. Three stood their ground and fired into the crowd. Several prisoners fell, instantly subsumed by the shoes of the rest as they continued toward the guards, who were effortlessly overpowered by the mob.

Three inmates took the weapons from the overpowered soldiers, and trained them on the fleeing guards. They fired but, due to recoil and darkness, only hit one guard, who fell into the mire with a wet thud.

Most of the escapees ran in the opposite direction, across the farm in a bid for freedom. Few were able to keep their feet, slipping and sliding in the mud, getting up, continuing to run, and repeating.

Those few who remained were now led by the three with weapons. They ran to the soldier they had cut down a moment before, taking his gun as well.

Four armed, and eight following, they advanced on the heading in which the soldiers had fled.

Shortly, gunfire stopped their advance. The soldiers had taken up a defensive position, where they outnumbered the armed prisoners.

Several flares were fired into the air, illuminating the area in blood-red ambience.

All the facility's lights were doused except a spotlight, trained on the escapees, and the flare-light.

"Lay down your weapons now, or we will fire on you," an amplified voice boomed from the camp's public address system.

Without hesitation, the prisoners fired into the darkness in the direction of the sound.

Targets clearly visible in the flare-light, the soldiers let bullets fly from their cover of darkness, momentarily revealing themselves by the flashes as their weapons discharged.

The armed prisoners were killed immediately in the withering hail, as were two of those who had followed them. The others were injured. All were sprawled in the mud, defeated.

Floodlights came on. Soldiers carrying first-aid cases ran to the assistance of their fallen comrades. Others crept gingerly to the dead and injured prisoners, taking care despite their apparent complete victory.

Lights were shone all around the camp. When trained on the centre of the facility, most of the prisoners were visible, hands raised, standing huddled together, so as to appear as harmless as possible. The number of those who had stayed inside was much smaller than the hundred who had escaped.

The small minority lay dead in the waning flarelight, while the runaways continued their sprint for freedom in the darkness and mud and were soon rounded up without resistance.

Marley reclined on his single bed, fingers interlocked behind his head, his face wet with tears. "Is this our fault?"

Sitting on a chair, Euan said nothing as he stared out the window of their twin hotel room at the bleak urban landscape. His eyes were cast down, a damp handkerchief in his hand.

"I mean, didn't we basically incite them to this? All that talk about their rights. Some experts we are. They insisted on their rights alright, and now we don't know how many are dead. That's what we achieved. Even the ones who didn't fight probably won't get amnesty now."

Euan looked up, gazing at the bland art print on the magnolia wall of their hotel room. His eyes were red and his muscles knotted. "Remember what that guy, Stanton, said? 'D'you think I actually feel anything for those cops?' We didn't create that. Those soldiers – or at least that one – were out for blood. He was inciting them."

"Okay, so they're responsible too. That doesn't change our part in it."

"I know. I'll take it to my grave." Euan squeezed his handkerchief as if trying to wring the tears from it.

"That makes two of us." Marley pressed his fingers to his closed eyelids, massaging more tears from them.

"But that doesn't change the facts. Those prisoners were being pressured to do… something. From two directions: us, and the soldiers." He looked at Marley. "That's no co-incidence. We've been used."

"What? Who would want to do that?"

"I don't know," Euan said, his voice low and gravelly. "But I mean to find out. What about you?"

The end of Send Him Victorious Book 2.
The story continues in Book 3, available now.

Thank You For Reading!

Dear Reader,

I hope you enjoyed *Send Him Victorious*. It is a story I have wanted to tell for a long time. I love my characters, and I hope that you do too. Is this the end of the road for them? Perhaps not. There are stories yet to tell concerning the British New Order.

God willing, I will write more of this series. I have huge things planned in this epic saga of my royal family and the world they inhabit.

I love feedback. While this is the story I wanted to tell, I did not write it just for me. I want to know what you liked, what you loved, even what you hated. I'd love to hear from you. You can connect with me at www.facebook.com/b.cline.author. Please like my page and offer some comments, opinions, and questions.

Finally, I need to ask a favour. If you're so inclined, I'd love a review of *Send Him Victorious*. Loved, hated, or indifferent, I'd just enjoy your feedback. Reviews can be tough to come by these days, and you, the reader, have the power to make or break a book. If you have the time, please leave a review at goodreads.com, your blog, and your favourite online retailer.

Thank you for reading *Send Him Victorious* and for spending time with me.

With gratitude,

Bart Cline